The Kimbo
– Stop the Presses! –
Series

Book Three

Antie EM

S.L. Kotar & J.E. Gessler

Ahead of The Press
St. Louis, MO

Library of Congress Cataloguing-in-Publication Data
The Kimbo – Stop the Presses! – Series Book 2 Antie EM
/ S.L. Kotar and J.E. Gessler

ISBN   KINDLE Mobi   978-1-950392-65-0   (ebook)
ISBN   PAPERBACK   978-1-950392-64-3

Ahead of The Press Publishing
St. Louis, Missouri

Table of Contents

The Kimbo - Hold the Presses! - Series

"Auntie EM"

Book III

Dedication

This novel is dedicated to Josephine Campbell, my cherished aunt. She was always very kind to me and always there when I needed her. She was a pioneering woman who took life by the horns and never knew the meaning of the word quit. I loved her very much and it's a pleasure, finally, to have this dedication in print, for I promised her a long time ago.

SLK

And JEG, always

ACT 1

It was sweltering in London. The temperature was 80 degrees and everyone was walking around as though the world were coming to an end. Men, ties loosened and tongues lolling from between polished teeth, looked more like poorly mannered Corgis than executives. Women fanned themselves with newspaper sections from the London *Times,* while exchanging business attire for short skirts the size of postage stamps.

The kind without a depiction of the Queen.

I seemed to be the only one unaffected by this unexpected global broiling. To me, 80 degrees was just about right. Having been born in a cold state, I disliked being too chilled; while having recently arrived in the United Kingdom from St. Louis, Missouri, U.S. of A., anything under 120 degrees and 100 percent humidity was heaven.

The reason *I* happened to have my tie untied and strung around my neck like a hempen noose prop out of a grade B, Western, was that I happened to be in the flat of my stringer, co-worker and dear friend, Gypsy.

My name, by the way, is Kimbo. A. Kimbo for lone and Andy for short. The reason I'm in England is because the wire service I work for, CANS, was transferred, kit and caboodle, from the Gateway City, to London. CANS, by the way, is the acronym for the Carry-All News Service. It's sort of like Reuters and UPI. Sort of, as in a guppy is sort of like a whale.

A guppy and a whale both live in water and have fins. CANS and UPI both gather news and sell it to newspapers. The difference being, Captain Ahab never lost a leg to an aquarium-sized tropical fish and CANS never sold a story to any Pulitzer-prize winning paper.

You'll hear that a lot as we go along; Pulitzer prize. It's a favorite expression of mine. When I say something is Pulitzer-prize, it's big. Really big. Bigger than big; bigger than Priceline.com, if you know what I mean. And, unlike some of my more jaded counterparts at other news services, I never, *ever* use the expression "Pulitzer prize" with anything less than total, absolute respect.

That's because I don't own one.

I don't have a Nobel peace prize either, but I'm not so eager to put one of those little trophies around my neck. I figure if Jimmy Carter doesn't have one, it's not worth owning. But a Pulitzer is another thing, entirely.

If I had one of those babies to call my own, I could write my own ticket.

Which is what I do, every three or four years. I wear out my welcome and write my own ticket out of town. That's a quote from my current editor, Sweet McGraw. He ought to know. He's fired me a few times.

None of them ever justified, by the way.

It just happens. I write a story, he wants it changed. I refuse; we negotiate. I move around a few semicolons, dot my "i's" and promise to mind my "P's" and "Q's." He prints the story, the newspaper gets sued or the local fuzz come breathing down on his neck and I'm outta there.

I have been called (in kinder, gentler moments) a Rolling Stone.

Actually, I would rather be the fifth Beatle, but I don't have any musical talent to speak of. I can whistle pretty well and can drum my fingers in time to the music, but as Pete Best can tell you, it takes more than that.

One thing I wouldn't have to worry about: I'm not better looking than Paul McCartney. I've never broken any mirrors, but his status as the Pretty Beatle would never be challenged with me in the band.

It wasn't with Pete, either, but losing out on fame and a couple of billion dollars tends to make a man bitter.

I was lounging around in Gypsy's flat, my legs slung over the arm of a chair, contemplating the joy of doing nothing, when she interrupted me out of my reverie.

"Listen to this," she began. I could tell I wasn't going to like what I heard because she had that suspicious tone in her voice. "They're taking up a collection to put lights around the Arch! I will send money."

The "Arch," as everyone knows, is in St. Louis. Missouri. Midwest. Bible Belt. "A Northern State with a Southern accent." You know where it is: between the "Land of Lincoln" and Dodge City.

I'm not from Missouri, by the way. I just tarried there long enough to collect a paycheck or two, watch a lot of baseball (prior to July 7, 1990), sniff around Dog Town a little and grow to loathe the Arch.

I swung my legs off the arm, settling them down with a resounding thump.

"You will not send money."

"But the writer says it's important that the Arch be lighted. Like the Washington Monument. He says the effect will be mesmerizing."

I groaned. Gypsy and I share a lot in common. We're both unusually bright, intuitive people. We care about what's happening in the world around us. I make my living writing about crime, murder and mayhem, while she makes her living telling fortunes and communing with dead spirits. I run a number of informants, known in the vernacular as "stringers." She consults a crystal ball.

One thing we do not share, however, is a fascination for the Arch. For those of you unfamiliar with St. Louis, the Arch is a silly monument planted, like an upside down horseshoe, on the St. Louis side of the Mississippi River. The rationale being, the city was called the Gateway to the West around the time Ward Bond was conducting wagon trains through the Great Plains.

In reality, it more closely resembles one half of that other famous, yellow arch, but you can't get a Big Mac under it.

The arch is supposed to symbolize this mythological "gate."

You'll hear a lot about mysticism if you read on, by the way.

That's because Gypsy really is a Gypsy. A real-life, honest Injun, Maria Ouspenskaya-palm reading, star-gazer. She helped me crack a big case involving a Mystic Seer and a stock market scandal. She also saved my life on another case by rescuing me from a far more heinous crook – the Internal Revenue Service.

For some reason I can't fathom, Gypsy had developed a sick fascination for St. Louis' symbol. Had she lived in that city for any length of time, I would have suspected Arch poisoning. Photos of the Arch are everywhere, from the pages of calendars to the names of dry cleaning stores. Visitors come from as far away as Illinois to see the Arch, while locals, traveling from trendy West County to work in the city, are often stuck in traffic on highway 40 long enough to sketch the Arch from memory – inch by inch.

Visitors leaving St. Louis view it in their rear view mirrors while dodging piles of uncollected garbage across the river in East St. Louis. (East St. Louis is in Illinois, by the way, just as surely as Kansas City is in Missouri.)

The first time I drive through St. Louis in the spring of 1982 (on my way to Los Angeles), my first impression of the city was that it had a great baseball team and a silly arch. My last impression of the city, as I was winging my way east toward Europe, was that it had a lousy baseball team and a silly arch.

Perhaps because I always harped on it, Gypsy sort of fell in love with The Arch. I guess she thought of it as unappreciated. Which is true enough, to go by me. I did try to explain there where a host of celebrities, like the mayor, whose political position made it expedient to adore it, so she needn't feel it required adoption (like the elephants at the Zoo), but it was too late. She had this "love affair" with the Arch and that was that.

I wasn't jealous of the Arch. I just didn't get it. Some girls go for teddy bears, some for movie stars. Mine just happened to go for a monument. That said, I will acknowledge the Arch is an architectural wonder. If we were still counting them, it'd be the Ninth or Tenth Wonder of the World. Constructing it from the ground up and making the two sides meet at the top was, I'm told, pretty darned impossible. It's hollow inside and you can take a cable car to the top where there's a platform you can look out from. And what do you see? St. Louis City on one side, the Mighty Mississippi either flooded or dry enough to walk over depending on the mood of federal river management engineers (Robert E. Lee, West Point graduate, was one of them in his day as a Union man, if that tells you anything), and East St. Louis, Illinois.

Stunning, really.

Not.

"I am not a 'girl,'" she corrected, reading my mind. She had an annoying habit of doing that, even though I had ordered her not to. It was part and parcel of her trade, and telepathy was second nature to her. But it had a way of getting under a guy's skin.

"My apologies," I muttered through gritted teeth. I'm usually more politically correct than that, but I was mad. There had to better things for two adults to argue over.

Like Northern Ireland or Jerusalem.

"Picture this," Gyp read to me from the *Post-Dispatch,* the one-horse newspaper in the Gateway City, which Sweet had delivered (slow boat rate) to the CANS office in London for *auld lang syne*). "'A warm, breezy spring night. Small tables are set up outside a downtown restaurant. As you and your companion enjoy your meal, lively music wafts through the air. As you look east, you see the Arch sparkling with multi-colored lights, a symbol of stability for those who live here.'"

"True," I agreed, picking my teeth with a fingernail. "If I ever saw it quivering, I'd know the New Madrid (pronounced Mah-drid, as opposed to Madrid, like in "Spain,") Fault was cracking, and run like hell."

Having spent a number of years on the West Coast, you better believe I knew all about "stability." Or lack thereof.

"'In Paris, the Eiffel Tower is illuminated as well, a source of pride for Parisians. The thought of the Arch shining brightly at night like that is downright exhilarating.'"

I picked on a scab while arching an eyebrow.

"Is that what the article says, or are you making it up as you go?"
She ignored me.

"'Soaring 630 feet above the Mississippi River, the Arch is one of St. Louis' greatest assets.'"

"Yeah," I agreed. "It sure isn't the baseball team." It's no secret I'm a Whitey Herzog fan and I'll never be happy until he comes back. His so-called retirement has ruined the game for me.

"'It is something most St. Louisans are proud of.'"

"It is something of which most St. Louisans are proud," I corrected. There are few things on earth a writer likes better than to correct another writer's work. Grammar included.

"'As St. Louisans struggle with the best ways to revitalize downtown and unite the region, they should consider throwing their full support behind efforts to light the Arch.' It will take forty 3,000-watt lights to make it work," she added, finally looking up and catching my illuminated smile. "They tested it."

"How much to pay for the electricity?" I inquired, Grinch-like.

"$14,000 a year."

I choked. Not enough to fund a research project to cure cancer, but nevertheless, a substantial amount.

Think of how many free Bi-State bus tickets they could issue to housekeeping personnel so they could get to work without having to spend any of their $5.00-an-hour salary on transportation.

Did I tell you Ralph Nader was my hero? At least he was, before he gave the election to Dubya.

I'm a 60's kind of guy. Not a "baby boomer," but someone who remembers what all the demonstrations were about; who participated in the first Earth Day; who wept when Man set foot on the moon. I guess you could call me a dreamer. Always was. Well, when you're born an unwanted kid and grow up in various and sundry orphanages, you get to be that way. It's called survival.

If anything, I'm a survivor.

I believe in fair play. That's my middle name. Andy "Fair Play" Kimbo.

I'm an atavism, a throwback to the days of the Lone Ranger. It's not that I see everything in whites and blacks: No one knows how grey a world can look more than I can. It's just that if there isn't some sort of justice in this life, it isn't worth living. Someone has to make the bad guys accountable for their misdeeds, be it violence, corruption or a disregard for the planet.

That's why I'm an investigative reporter. Because I think people have the right to know the truth. I never subscribed to the theory, "what you don't know won't hurt you." On the contrary, it's what They choose not to say which can eventually destroy – not only you, in the smaller sense, but us – in the larger context.

Do I think there's substantial proof of live on Mars? You betcha I do. It may not be Elvis, but it's there, and no one is saying so because the Radical Right would freak out, go stark raving mad. Go ahead and interpret The Book any way you want, but don't lay your fears on me. If your world falls apart, that's your problem. Adapt or die. That's Darwinism and it's me, too.

The phone rang and I didn't make a move to answer it. It wasn't my flat and no one knew I was here. I presumed the caller was one of Gypsy's clients, ringing 'round for a chat about dear olde dad, and where he hid the keys to the treasure cabinet before passing on to his reward.

"Hello?" Gypsy inquired into the mouthpiece. When she nodded gravely, I knew my hunch had been right. "Just a minute." To my astonishment, she held out the phone to me. "It's for you."

"I don't communicate with the dead," I protested.

I could hear the voice on the other end as clearly as though I'd had the phone to my ear.

"I'm not dead and if you don't speak to me, Kimbo, you're going to wish you were."

That was enough to arch both my eyebrows. Any more of this and I've be asking if he wanted fries with his order.

I took the instrument of torture and held it in close proximity to my ear.

"What are you doing, calling me at this number?" I demanded of my editor, Sweet McGraw. "No one's supposed to know I'm here. I'm off duty," I added for form's sake.

"The hell you are. I want you."

"Uncle Sam you're not," I argued.

"I need someone to watch the switchboard tonight. You're it, Kimbo."

As in, "tag, you're it." But I never was much for games playing, especially juvenile ones. I hadn't much practice.

"Where's Rita?"

"In Paris, on assignment."

That figured. Rita was the auntie of the CANS office. She got sent to Paris because Sweet figured she wouldn't have anything better to do there but work.

"Where's Jimbo?"

"He went to cover the Monaco 500."

Jimbo knew as much about car racing as he did about sentience. I had once accused him of being as dull as dish water and he had thanked me for the compliment.

"What about *you?*"

"I have a sore throat. I want to go home and go to bed."

I didn't want to go home but I could sympathize with the rest.

"Put the answering machine on," I suggested. "No one ever calls us with any hot-breaking stories. I think the enormity of the remuneration scares them off."

"Very funny," Sweet snorted.

Mr. Harold Poxie (rhymes with "epoxy"), the owner of CANS, believed news ought to be free. That meant anyone giving us a hot tip should do so out of the goodness of his or her own heart. Which was why the switchboard never rang at night, unless it was a bill collector. Those people never sleep. They're like cockroaches. You get one and the rest move in. One finds your telephone number and pretty soon it's like you're running Ma Bell out of your home. Or office.

Of course, Mr. Poxie doesn't practice what he preaches, or he'd have to give the stories his reporters dig up to his wire service subscribers without charge.

If he did that, he wouldn't be able to afford a second Rolls Royce and I'd be out of a job. Again.

"Sweet," I tried. "You sound fine to me. Take two aspirin and call me in the morning."

"You're not a doctor," he groused. "Get over here in half an hour so I can go home to bed."

"OK," I agreed. Too readily.

"And don't think you can wait until I'm out of sight, then turn the answering machine on and leave. I'm going to call you and if I get that damned tape recording, you're out on your ass. And don't think Mr. Poxie will fly you home, either. You'll have to paddle your way back on a raft."

"Thanks a lot," I growled and hung up. Gypsy looked at me with cat-soft eyes. "Why didn't you use your mind reading act to see who that was on the phone before you answered it?" I demanded.

"Oh," she laughed lightly. "I knew who it was."

"Then why did you pick up the handset?"

"He has a sore throat."

I stared at her in dumb stupefaction.

"So what?"

"Besides, I will be busy. I have to write a letter."

"A letter? To whom?"

"To the man taking up a collection to light the Arch."

If she meant to get rid of me in one hell of a hurry, she succeeded beyond her wildest dreams.

"Good night," I muttered from between clenched teeth. She stopped me as I reached the door.

"Shall I send cash or should I write a check?"

I hesitated, allowing an evil smile to decorate my handsome, movie star face. You could tell I was feeling better.

"Send cash. A twenty pound note would be lovely."

Then I hightailed it out of there before she could read my mind. No one in St. Louis would know an English twenty pound note from fool's gold. They'd think it was funny money and throw it out.

I left, shutting the door behind me. It was nice to know I had perpetrated at least one good deed today.

ACT 2

Had I been in the States, the drive from Gypsy's flat to the CANS office building would have taken twenty minutes. In London, the evolving capital city of Europe, it took closer to an hour. Even at this time of night, the metropolis was crawling with life. I passed men with purple hair and bald women; natives wearing street-length, brightly-colored India dresses, or mini-skirts so skimpy they doubled for G-strings.

Tourists wore T-shirts proclaiming "I Love London," "Nessie Lives" and "Stonehenge Forever," while walking in that prison-shuffle developed by those passport-wielding people whose arms are perpetually laden down with packages they will ultimately try to convince customs officials were bought in Hoboken.

In fact, the only people dressed in business attire were the naturalized citizens who came from such far-away places as South Africa, India and Wales.

While it was once proclaimed the sun never set on the British Empire, it may now be said that the suns sets, all right, but no one notices it.

I'm not usually a man who demands perks as a term of employment, but when informed I was being transferred to England, I did scream, yell, curse and otherwise act in a rational manner when begging for a car. Actually, they're referred to as a "motor" here, much in the same manner as people investing money in Lloyds of London are referred to as "Names."

The similarity is clear: the "motors" run on rubber bands attached to hamsters and the "Names" have the pleasure of admiring their pretend genealogy while filing for bankruptcy.

My automobile was made in the Czech Republic, or whatever it's called these days. It has two doors which stick, four reasonably round tires, a braking system fashioned after the piece of wood that serves as a brake on a kid's go-cart, and an unadvertised sun roof, created after getting the car up to fifty miles an hour and having the roof fly off.

The one thing this car excels at is petrol *consumption,* which is something like the disease of the same name they make you take a skin test for before you can get a job. Like TB, which gobbles up your lungs, my motor drank fuel at the ratio of one kilometer to three liters of gas. At two pounds a liter, that makes it a pretty expensive ride.

(Note: in the U.K. they use the anti-American metric system.)

And then there's the parking problem. Which is to say, there is no parking. By the time you deposit your motor in a garage and walk to your destination, you discover it would have been easier to simply hike from where you were, to where you're going, without having driven at all.

But there was one good thing to say about London. It didn't have an Arch.

Make that two things. It didn't have a lousy baseball team, either.

I arrived at the formally condemned office building CANS rented for its London-based wire service and let myself in the front door. While I had a key, I found it easier to use a piece of celluloid and slip it up, between lock and door. It was an old trick I learned while working in Los Angeles. There, in the spirit of recycling, rather than trash a turkey movie, they sold it to cable. After the cable company got through shredding it, there were mounds of film reels lying about. My strip of film came from *Naked in New York.* As a movie, it made a great lock pick.

The building was deserted. There was supposed to be a security guard on duty, but wasn't. With an eye toward fiscal responsibility, the human being was replaced by a sign, warning: Danger. Night Watchman.

I knew he didn't exist, because one night I left out a bottle of J&B. The next morning it was still there. I call it the 98-full-proof test.

The lease also guaranteed two surveillance cameras on the premises at all times. It didn't specify they had to be working, however, and like the majority of the building staff, they weren't.

There were two elevators, called "lifts" which you could take to the penthouse, or top floor, where the CANS wire service did business. I took the stairs. I'm not a health nut and I don't enjoy flirting with a coronary every time I go to work. It's just that I would rather have a heart attack on the back stairs, than perish stuck between floors in an elevator. Or turned into strawberry-colored Jell-O after the lift failed to live up to its name.

I could hear Sweet pacing, sweaty and out of breath as I emerged from the stair well. By the way he was grumbling, his sore throat was the least of his problems.

"There you are!" he greeted in typical editor fashion. Not, "Thank God you got here all right, Andy," or "Kimbo, you're a sight for sore throats." Just, "There you are!" It make me feel welcome and extraneous at the same time.

He was a great editor, a man from the Old School. And he wasn't wearing a tie, to prove it.

"Here I am," I agreed, sidling away from him, lest he come up and breathe on me. If he really were coming down with a cold, I didn't want to catch it. He misinterpreted my evasive action.

"Whatsamatter?" he growled. "You think I'm funny, or something?"

"Yes, sir," I agreed with one of my patented, charming smiles. "I laugh myself nearly to death every time I get my paycheck."

"It doesn't look any better than mine."

Which was so close to the truth, he made me laugh, despite myself.

"Go home, Sweet. Drink a quart of orange juice and crawl into bed. You'll be amazed how well you feel in the morning."

"I may be dying," he predicted.

"In that case, soak your feet."

"What does that have to do with my illness?"

The rationale was clear to me, but a little difficult to explain to someone else. Where I was raised, there were only three remedies to cover a multitude of illnesses: forcing fluids, soaking the effected part, or a good slug of calomel. I didn't think he'd appreciate the latter, so I opted for the first two. If drinking and soaking didn't work, then a kid (or a man) was a goner.

It all had to do with hyrdopathy and water being cheap.

Calomel was a last ditch effort, resorted to only in cases of chicken pox and when the State inspector made rare, unannounced visits.

Or when the Army recruiter came calling. It was presumed he was well versed in sticking things in and receiving things out of the areas calomel affected.

The orphanages and foster homes of my acquaintance made a pretty lively business selling "spanking clean" boys into the armed forces. The only reason I escaped a similar fate was by permanently absenting myself after my sixteenth birthday. They looked for me all right, but I had made a study of successful prison breaks. Unlike my counterparts who had bolted into the wilderness and been tracked down by the blood hounds, I headed right for the biggest city I could find. The dogs couldn't track me there and with a cap pulled low over my tell-tale red hair, I was just another child labor law refugee.

"Hard Work" is my middle name. I never minded putting my nose to the grindstone and earning my keep. I've done a lot of things in my life, not a lot of them pretty. But I survived and that's the name of the game.

Isn't it?

"Are you listening to me?" Sweet was demanding. I came out of my fog and nodded less than enthusiastically. If I overplayed my hand, he would know I was lying.

"Yeah. I heard every word."

"Then remember it," he warned over his shoulder as he stepped into the lift.

I wished him bon voyage.

There were two overhead lights burning in the office. I snapped both off, then lit the small banker's lamp on my desk. The green glass shade cast a dull, otherworldly shadow over a ten centimeter area, just enough to keep the dark away.

I didn't want to be disturbed by boogie men while I slept.

I didn't get to sleep long. By my reckoning, I had just stretched my legs out and closed my eyes – to rest them, you understand – when the phone rang. It scared the heebie jeebies out of me, and I jumped like a cat on a hot tin roof. Cursing Sweet for being inconsiderate, I yanked up the receiver and started to growl into the mouth piece. Then I remembered who was on the other end (who else could it be?) and changed my tune. If that SOB thought he had caught me napping, fur would fly. I therefore determined to shock him. Putting on my best bedroom voice, I purred into the phone.

"Carry-All News Service, Kimbo speaking. How may I help you?"

There was a long pause on the other end and I smiled, imagining Sweet had taken a powder over my professionalism. But when the guy on the other end spoke, it was I who flipped.

"Say, can you give me the time?"

The caller was hesitant, almost confused. In my instantly irritated state, I attributed his reticence to an overdose of wood alkie.

"Check your watch," I advised, or something to that effect, punctuated with four-letter words.

"It isn't working."

"What do you think I am – Big Ben, for crying out loud?" No answer. "Stick your head out the window next time it chimes and count 'em," I ungraciously advised.

"My watch stopped," the called whined. My heart was breaking.

"So – wind it."

"It runs on a battery."

"What do you think I am – a jeweler? When the shops open, go out and buy a battery. They cost about two bucks."

The hesitation was longer this time.

"What's a buck?"

I had forgotten idiomatic phrases do not translate well.

"A male deer. And if you want to know where I'd like to insert an antler just about now –"

"You don't understand," the man pursued, this time with a trace of pique in his voice. "I'm wearing a Rolex watch. The battery is less than a year old. It can't have worn down. To avoid that unpleasantness, I buy a new Rolex every year."

"Yeah," I sympathetically commiserated. "To match the color of your new Rolls Royce."

"My Jaguar, actually," he corrected. "But you don't seem to understand. The radio-controlled mechanism in my Rolex is guaranteed for life."

Which would get the manufacturer off the hook if I could get my hands around this guy's neck.

"So – sue for restitution."

"Sue" was one word which was comprehended in any language.

I had almost decided to hang up on the jerk when he spoke again. Putting the earpiece closer to my head so I could hear him, I asked him to repeat what he just said.

"There's something queer going on."

Now, "queer" is a funny word – no pun intended. To most people, it means "deviate," as in sexual behavior. To yours truly, however, it signifies *news.*

"Could you be more specific?"

"Everything's stopped working. My television, my radio, my computer."

"A power failure –" And then I remembered the watch wasn't driven by electricity. Not the plugged-in kind, anyway.

"Everything," he stressed.

"And you're worried about your *watch?"*

"I'm worried about time."

He said, "I'm worried about time." Not, "I'm worried about *the* time." Or, "I'm worried about what time it is." An odd way to phrase his sentence. Unless he meant exactly what he said.

I'm a writer; words are my stock and trade. Putting aside the fact everyone in the U.K. talks a little funny, this man's statement was decidedly peculiar.

I tried a little fake.

I had a wind-up Timex. I'm from the Old School, remember? Takes a lickin' and keeps on tickin'. It hadn't lost more than a minute in the last decade. I identified with their 1950's advertising. I could have been their poster boy. And then I remembered. I had left it on Gypsy's bedside stand.

"It's 1:03," I lied.

"Thank you." Then, "Can you tell me what's happening?"

"No. I can't."

"I need help."

I was running out of patience, just as fast as he was running out of time. We were in a foot race and I was determined to come out ahead.

"With your watch?"

"About time."

"Nothing has happened to time. Old Father Time is on the job as usual, I assure you. He's not eligible for Social Security, and his employer doesn't provide a pension, so I expect he'll be there until the end of – *time,"* I added.

I'm often accused of having a mean streak. I deny it, but, of course, am secretly flattered whenever so incriminated.

"Don't you care?"

If he had said anything else, anything else at all, the egg timer would have signaled him soft boiled. But by asking if I cared, he hit me in my weak spot. Trouble is, you see, I do care. About a lot of things, not the least of which are the obscure, off-the-wall things no one else gives a fig about.

"Yes," I guardedly replied. "I do care."

"Can you come over here?"

"Where is 'here'?" I asked, feeling more fool than reporter. It's a disease I've suffered from since I earned my first Jimmy Olsen, Cub Reporter badge.

"I'm down below, actually," he admitted, with that guilty tone of voice which made me believe he didn't want me to think he was some sort of tramp. "My mobile wouldn't work, so I went to the garage to use my car phone."

He gave me an address in the ritzy part of London. That confirmed the Rolex and the Jaguar.

"OK," I agreed. "Hurry home from your gahr-radge," I tried in dialect. I can meet you at your pad in forty-five minutes."

Never let it be said I don't deserve what I get.

"How will I know when that is?"

His watch wasn't working.

"When I ring on your doorbell."

"It's not working."

My shoulders sagged.

"I'll knock!"

"Thank you."

"What's your name, by the way?" I inquired, jotting down some notes as we talked.

"Edgar Highsmyth Rollins-McMurtry, IV."

"Yes, sir. Got it. I'll be right there –"

"Not *Sir,*" he corrected in that chipped, upper-crust voice they breed into these boys at conception. "Actually, I am an earl."

"Earl? I thought you said your name was Ed?"

"'Earl' is my title."

He was making me nostalgic for federal parks with upside-down horseshoes and mighty rivers you can wade across during droughts.

"Right-O, Eddie baby. How do I get past the door-shaker?"

That was the thing about reporters. We all talked like we covered the Lindbergh baby kidnapping. Personally. It was a fraternity thing, but without the silly handshakes and code names comprised of Greek letters.

"What's a door shaker?"

"The security guard," I explained in words of one syllable, as though he were an idiot. Which he might very well have been, for all I knew.

"I shall send word down to have you admitted."

For the life of me, if he had substituted "committed" for "admitted," I wouldn't have been surprised. This caper was sounding more and more like a wild goose chase all the time.

"Good. See you in a jiff, Mr. Earl."

I hung up the phone, started to put the answering machine on, then thought better of it. When Sweet did call to check up on me, he'd never believe I was out on assignment. Better just leave the phone off the hook. That way, I could always say I was interviewing Glenda Jackson, M.P. when he called.

She was, after all, a lot prettier than Prince Philip. And had nothing whatsoever to say about widget factories.

ACT 3

I never got to meet that guy with two first names and half a dozen last names. My motor, made in the Czech Republic, wouldn't start. I should have been suspicious, but wasn't. It ran on hamster-power but presumably needed an electric shock to get them started. So, I walked. By the time I got within two blocks of his up-town address, I ran into all kinds of problems.

Literally.

First of all, the traffic lights were out. Now, that's not as tragic as it sounds, for no one bothers to follow them, anyway. It was all the rest of the lights – the massive, multi-colored neon advertisements, the store names, the high-rise windows with their glaring announcements that, "I'm home; drop up and see me, sometime, big boy" that were haywire.

There were bobbies (cops), too, adding to the confusion. None of them carry guns over here, so to make up for that glaring deficit, they carried whistles. Two or three a piece, I guessed from the racket. Wave, wave, blow – blow, wave. It was like being caught in one gigantic dirty movie, if you know what I mean.

Raising my hand like the third-grader, I waved and hollered at one of the "coppers."

"What's going on here?"

"What's it look like?" he yelled back, giving me, I suppose, just what I deserved, for asking a stupid question.

Which inspired me to merge into the crowd and mingle with the natives who had come out of their flats to have a look at the confusion, first hand.

Lookie-loos, we call them in the States.

I, on the other hand, had a legitimate reason for being outside and adding to the general confusion. I was a reporter.

And I'd been called a lot worse things in my day than a lookie-loo.

Holding out my miniature tape recorder, I attempted to interview some of the more human-looking citizens.

"Andy Kimbo, Carry All News Service," I identified myself. "What's happening here?"

"It's the end of the world."

I tried another eye witness, just knowing Sweet would never let that particular quote go to press.

"Any idea what's going on?"

"It's an IRA attack."

"Was there a bomb?"

"Must have been."

"Anybody killed?"

He looked around eagerly for blood. I passed on. Figuratively.

"Hey – madam!" I called, hailing a tall, particularly attractive brunette who was hurrying away from me with that tell-tall aura of "I know more than you do." "Do you live around here?"

"Who's asking, dearie?" the person so accused asked in a falsetto, turning around and batting long eyelashes at me. It was neither the voice, nor the lack of cleavage which gave his gender away: it was the thick, curly chest hairs peering out from beneath the brassier. I swallowed. Nervously.

"Ron Smith," I quickly identified myself. "From UPI." Before I could say another word, he waved me off.

"Do you have the time?" he demanded, instead.

This was the second "time" in an hour someone had asked me the time. Considering I was no more than five foot eight inches in lifts, I hardly passed for a Big Ben look-alike.

"No," I pouted. "What's a'matter with your watch?"

"It stopped."

"When?"

"About an hour ago. I have an appointment to keep, and I have to be there exactly on time."

"Where were you an hour ago when your watch malfunctioned?"

"In the park," he indicated. "Talking to Albert. He's the bobby on patrol there," he added. I wasn't sure why and didn't pursue it. I'm a reporter, but that doesn't mean I'm nosey.

"Did you ask Albert for the time – when you noticed your watch wasn't working?"

"Yes," he nodded agreeably.

"Was his watch working?"

"He wasn't wearing one." My face fell. "But he did direct me to a repair shop across the way; there's a large clock in the window."

"Was it working?" I eagerly demanded.

"No. It wasn't. None of the clocks displayed in the window were working. That's odd, isn't it – that a watch repair shop would have broken clocks displayed in their window."

Odd was rapidly becoming the word of the moment.

"I bet they were all working right at midnight. Where did you say this shop was?"

He pointed me in the right direction, then scurried off, his pumps clickety-clacking on the hard sidewalk. I paused a moment to stare after him, wondering where he had gotten his designer outfit in a 44 tall, then hurried away.

Even a heathen like me knows you can't buy a Armani in a size larger than an 8 petite.

Working my way through the throng, I found the watch repair shop. Right enough, all the clocks had stopped. Snapping a photo, taking care not to include the owner's name in the frame, I paused to take stock of the situation.

Number One: wrist watches and electric clocks had all malfunctioned.

Number Two: traffic lights, neon lights, elevators, computers, door bells and all things electric had stopped working.

Question: what did they have in common?

Question: what kind of force, energy or power could disrupt them simultaneously?

Answer: I didn't know.

Plan: find out in one hell of a hurry.

I took a few more snapshots for the folks back home, then determined the next step was to find out the range of the disaster. Taking a cab was out of the question, so I started walking.

I walk a lot. Unlike my fellow earthlings, I don't consider walking a disgrace. You know what I mean: the guy in the Mercedes who jogs five miles a day will tour around the grocery parking lot for half an hour waiting until a space opens up right next to the door. Or, the woman who romps all morning to the Oldies will idle her minivan in the fire lane while she runs in and returns the rented videos.

The first motor vehicle I ever remember seeing was the beat up old truck which came to the orphanage to lug kids out to one of the local farms. We picked corn, berries, apples, whatever was in season, then were toted back the same way, exhausted and with a severe care of the runs. Since they didn't feed us, we ate whatever was growing in the fields.

Ever study in your history lessons about how the soldiers of the Confederacy ate green corn and apples because they were starving? And how disease wiped out more men than Minnie balls? Believe it.

The first car I ever drove was an old Dodge. I borrowed it without permission and took it for a joy ride. I didn't get very far, but it was a good lesson. Walking was not only safer, it was a lot faster.

The first official driving lesson I ever received was from a cross-country truck driver. I was hitchhiking and they guy stopped to pick me up. He wasn't doing it from the milk of human kindness: he wanted to sleep while someone else drove the truck. He put me behind the wheel, showed me where how the gear worked, then said to keep my eyes open and steer into the turns.

He need not have bothered with the advice about keeping my eyes open. I seriously doubt I blinked all the way through Kansas.

After that harrowing experience, I made myself a sign: Will drive for passage. I figured I was a pro. Worked OK, too; I did great on the straightaway. It wasn't until I hit the first town that I "ran into" trouble.

After that, I asked where the brake pedal was. Seemed I had pumped the hell out of the clutch.

For years I used a driver's license I had taken out of a wallet which conveniently happened to find its way into my sweaty palms. There were no photos on licenses in those days and I guess I looked as much like Abigail Addams as I did A. Kimbo.

I walked a mile of London streets before checking my watch. It was a habit, actually; I had forgotten I wasn't wearing one. Fortunately, there were dozens of wrist and pocket watches strewn about the street where they had been tossed in frustration. I picked up one of the latter. It had a freight train on the cover. That gave me the warm fuzzies. Using my thumbnail, I pried it under the lid and it popped up. That started a tinkle-tune. I tried to place it and finally came up with, "I've been working on the railroad all the livelong day." I figured it had belonged to an Chinese tourist from Utah. That's where they drove in the golden spike at the completion of the cross-continent line. To my surprise, I saw the second had sweeping merrily around the dial. Looking around, I noticed the traffic lights functioning. All right.

I turned back, this time keeping an eye on my pocket watch. Whenever it stopped working, I knew I had wandered back into the affected area. Jotting street names down in my handy-dandy pad, with my equally handy-dandy mechanical pencil, I made an entire circle. It was still too early to pop into a store and buy a road map, so I made my way back to the euphemism commonly known as my transportation, and took one out of the glove compartment.

Tracing my route, I pretty accurately determined the circumference of the disaster. It roughly equated to one square mile, or whatever the equivalent is in kilometers.

What in God's name could put the kibosh on a square mile of electronic equipment?

It was then I was thrown into a state of denial, of the kind you experience when the earth beneath your feet starts shaking. Everyone knows the earth doesn't tremble. Therefore, anyone caught in an earthquake first thinks the problem is with you, rather than the ground beneath your feet. It's only when the chandelier starts swaying that you believe what your senses are telling you.

And crawl under the dining room table.

Unless it happens to be one those pedestal types – you know, instead of having four legs, it has one big one in the middle? Has anyone ever sat at a pedestal dining room table and *not* had it shake so bad it caused ripples in the cream soup?

Don't get me wrong. I'm not against pedestal tables. In fact, I generally function better with one, inasmuch as I'm always kicking a dining room table leg, even if I'm seated in the middle, with people on either side of me. Lack of early training, I guess. It's like that damned European habit of eating with the fork in the left hand.

Can anyone tell me what the point is?

I can understand, if all you're going to do is hold the fork in the left hand while spearing the meat with a knife, and shoving it into your mouth with your right. That makes the fork useless, so it doesn't matter if you're there, white-knuckled, clutching it in your uncoordinated left hand, wondering how in God's name you're going to navigate to your mouth without hitting your nose by mistake.

Sort of like driving without lessons.

And now that I'm on the subject, why, oh why, do Europeans hold the fork *upside down,* for crying out loud?

It's no wonder we had a War for Independence. I seriously doubt the Revolution was about taxes on tea. What the Colonists really wanted was to break away from antiquated dining habits.

Can't you see this? Martha and George Washington are sitting at the dining room table, eating dinner. While she's demurely wiping her lips on a white linen napkin that nobody nowadays would dare use for fear of staining, she sees George fumble a bit of steak and kidney pie off that fork he's got in his left hand, tines pointed toward the floor. Horrified at his poor manners, she corrects him.

"Mr. Washington, I must ask you not to behave like a Commoner while eating. I am afraid you will set a poor example for our future progeny."

Embarrassed and annoyed, George throws his napkin down on their Early American dining room set and gets up.

"Mrs. Washington, I will not have you rebuke me at table."

"Like any good politician's wife, my dear, I am only trying to keep your name out of the tabloids. If you persist in displaying poor table manners, do you wish Henry Wadsworth Longfellow to write a famous poem immortalizing you, instead of that silversmith in his classic, The *Midnight Slide of Paul Revere?* Do you want everyone to read in the Colonial *Sun* that the future Father of Their Country is a uncouth bumpkin?"

"What does anyone named Wadsworth know about table manners?"

"Oh," she pooh-poohs, bringing a hand to her perfectly coiffured "do." "If you persist, you know that little ditty he is going to write:

> Listen, my children, and you shall hear
> about the culinary manners of Paul Revere.
>
> Fork is by left, knife is by right,
> Improperly seated at table and ready to bite.
>
> While I, on the opposite side shall be,
> ready to criticize the drop of a pea."

"Madam, 'Washington' does not rhyme with 'here.' It simply will not work."

She gave the subject its proper consideration and deftly corrected the first stanza.

> Listen my children, and before I am done
> you will hear of the slob named George Washing*ton.*

"Mrs. Washington, while it is a known fact that I am psychic and will have a dream predicting a terrible civil war between the North and the South, and that I will place in my will a stipulation that all slaves at Mt. Vernon be given their freedom in 1863, thus humiliating the Runner-Up for the starring part in 'Father of His Country, the Sequel,' you have no such talent.

"I must therefore ask you to stay in the background, smile, wave to the crowds and hold your tongue, thus setting an example for all future First Wives.

"Secondly, I will not be judged by the standards followed by a deranged king, ruling an island barely larger than Manhattan, and worth no more than a handful of beads and rattles. Given the first excuse –"

"Such as having to reside in the makeshift capitol in Philadelphia rather than the much more famous and properly designated future White House?"

"Exactly! I shall petition the Continental Con-*gress* to go to war. Down with Tippy Canoes and Table Manners, Too!"

"That is all very well, husband, but I have a question."

"I grant you permission to ask it."

"If you are to be known as the Father of His Country, who, then is to be the Mother of Her Country? And be careful how you answer. Two hundred years from now, that upstart inventor and erstwhile politician, Thomas Jefferson, will still be having problems explaining *his* part in populating the New World!"

"True, madam, only too true. But, it shall do my reputation no harm. While I will eventually free my slaves – after we have no further need of them – Jefferson will leave his in bondage. Including 'Mrs. Jefferson,' as the generals and I joke about at Valley Forge – and selling off their sons for a considerable profit to his heirs."

It's all very complicated, I grant you, but after the Great War that Began All Wars, Americans held forks in their right hands and began drinking diet Pepsi.

Of course, we lost out on the health craze, because everyone knows drinking tea helps prevent everything from cancer to enlarged prostates. But like George, I'm a skeptic. I know how these things go. In a few years, some group of researchers will come out and declare drinking tea causes the wings to drop off fruit flies.

And who would want to lose their wings?

Still shaking from the enormity of equating history to my present situation, I cranked up my rubber band-driven motor and drove back to the CANS office. Predictably, Sweet was waiting there for me.

"Where have you been?" he demanded, righteously indignant. "I give you one simple job to perform and as soon as my back is turned, you flutter out of here like a bee after the honey pot."

Maybe I *should* be worried about my wings....

"Pour me a cuppa and I'll explain," I gasped, out of breath from climbing 434 steps from ground level to the CANS penthouse.

"A cup of what?" he demanded.

"A cuppa." From his expression, I gathered he was sadly deficit on his foreign slang. "A cup of tea."

"Tea? We don't have any tea here. And if you want a cuppa coffee, you can pour it yourself!"

I guess he didn't have anything wrong with his prostate. But, of course, I didn't ask. Guys never ask other guys about such things.

It's bad luck.

After getting my java, I prostrated myself on his office couch.

"Where have I been all night?" I demanded. "I've been covering the biggest story to hit London since the abdication of George the Whatever and you slept through it."

He yawned and I hated him.

"You mean the traffic lights all being out? Who cares? This is Europe, remember? No one ever follows traffic lights." It was the glint in my eyes which gave me away. "Now, wait a minute, Kimbo! You're not going to tell me you suspect some nefarious plot behind traffic lights, are you?"

I smugly nodded.

"That I do, m'lord."

Sweet rolled his eyes, while waving his hands in the air.

"Why do reporters all talk as though they're frustrated playwrights? Can't you just say, 'Yup' like everyone else and be done with it? Why does everything out of your mouth have to be melodramatic?"

He was right, of course. As anyone who writes for a living can tell you, we're never satisfied in our chosen field. Screen writers all crave to be investigative reporters. That's why they're always doing movies dealing with current events and conspiracies about the deaths of famous people. Reporters are eaten up inside to pen the Great American Novel, and poets who don't get to be Laureates and eat off White House china just know their real avocation is to be a tunesmith.

But I ignored him.

That was also a trait common to all writers.

"Well, I don't see anything in it. I want you to cover the Anniversary of Princes Di's death. Now, that's real Human Interest."

Translated, that meant it sold newspapers.

"This story is bigger than that," I humbly demurred. (I was polite because I knew he was correct. No one cared about current events; not until they could watch it a decade later in the Cinema.)

Of course, Martin Sheen *is* better looking than most of our presidents....

"Sweet, listen to me. The anniversary of Princes Di's death ought to be covered from a woman's POV. (To those of you unfamiliar with script writing terminology, that means 'point of view'.) Have Rita cover it."

"Rita isn't a woman, she's an old lady," he pointed out. "Besides, she's in Paris. I want you to get out in the street; interview the common man; get her feelings. Write a real tear-jerker."

I wanted to point out that Sweet was gender incorrect, but remembered he was from the Old School.

(Excuse the frequent use of Capital Letters, by the way. Everyone in the e.u. capitalizes Everything, except that which ought to be capitalized. Fortunately, i would Never fall into such a Trap.)

"I'm telling you this is big. Really Big."

"A power outage is Big?"

"It wasn't just a power outage; it was..."

"Don't say it," he moaned. I overlapped his protest.

"Weird."

"I knew you'd say it."

"It's more than a power outage. Look: I traced its effect. One square mile. What kind of routine, ordinary power outage affects one square mile?" I hurried on as he faltered. "If 'British Electric' had really gone out, the power would have been lost for miles and miles – a whole grid of electricity would have died."

I could see he liked the word "died." It had real saleable potential.

"And it wasn't only the electricity," I hurried on. "Even things powered by batteries went haywire. I was talking to this guy on the phone –"

"What guy?"

"I don't know. Some guy with thirty-six last names. He called here, wanting to know what had happened to time."

"At least he answered the phone," Sweet muttered, more for his own sake than mine.

"His Really Expensive Watch wasn't working. A watch which runs on a battery. It was cuckoo. His cell phone didn't work, either. He had to call me from his car phone."

"Poor bastard. My heart bleeds for him."

"Mine, too. But don't you see what I'm getting at? Everything which ran on electricity or a battery went out of order."

"Then, why did the phone in his car work?"

My eyes popped out of their sockets. I thought fast.

"He said it was in the parking *gahr-radge.*"

"The what?"

"Garage," I lamely translated. "Maybe it was so far underground it wasn't affected."

Sweet stopped in mid protest, mouth hanging open. With all the flies in the office, I didn't think that was such a good idea, so I hurried on.

Especially given that you catch more flies with Sweet than you do with Sour.

"You have to ask yourself, 'What's going on?' So I did."

"What was the answer?"

"I don't know."

"That'll make a great story. They'll love us on Downing Street. CANS News Service declares a State of Emergency but can't explain Weird Phenomenon. Do they still behead people in this country for causing a panic?"

"No. They eliminated capital punishment right after they executed John Reginald Christie, who killed all the people they hanged Timothy John Evans for murdering."

I could see he was clearly impressed.

"I like a reporter who does his background work. Good boy, Andy."

I didn't have the heart to tell him I heard learned those salient facts from *10 Rillington Place.* It was a John Hurt, Richard Attenborough film.

I wished I had written it.

It's probably the best film you've never seen.

Story of my life.

"So," I prodded. "Can I cover it? Please? Pretty please with sugar on top?"

Guys hate to see other guys beg.

Another one of those guy things I find useful from Time to Time.

"All right. But don't make something out of nothing. If it proves to be a dead issue, then drop it."

"And cover Princes Di's death. Right. I got you."

Sweet seemed satisfied, so I lit out of there faster than a bee after a honey pot.

Congratulating myself that I made no comment about the other meaning of honey pot.

Which had nothing whatsoever to do with Winnie the Pooh.

ACT 4

London is the new melting pot of Europe. No, let me rephrase that. All this talk about "pot" is likely to get me into trouble.

London is the new cosmopolitan capital of Europe. Lacking only the irrepressible magic of the Beatles, it's the 1960's all over again. The standards for music, entertainment, fashion and cuisine are all being dictated by the English. Even the Americans are listening.

So you know the scene has to be pretty loud.

Which is why I had to raise my voice to be heard over the music blaring in the background of the trendy cafe (do they still use the word "trendy"?) I slipped into after the opening bell had sounded.

La Boutique was a little of everything except a hairdressing salon, or a knickknack shop, which the name implied. They served expresso coffee by the pot ("I swear to you, officer, I'm clean!"), served brioche with unsalted butter, and if you have the bad taste to mention "fish and chips," they'll think you're referring to an off-the-wall rock an' roll band.

"So, tell me," I began, snapping on my transistor tape recorder. "What's it all about?"

The person to whom I addressed my comment made an obscure remark in an even more obtuse language and walked away. It appears I had mistaken the long flowing robes and nose ring as a waiter's outfit, when they actually belonged to another patron.

"Sorry," I apologized.

That was another thing about London. With a population of 7 million, about one tenth of that claimed some other language as their native tongue.

Which didn't mean they weren't born in England. On the contrary, most of them were second or third generation Brits. It's just that they found it more – expressive – to maintain an Old World flavor in this Brave New World of castles, dungeons and state-of-the-art observatories which look like amusement park rides.

"Anyone here have a guess about the power outage?" I shouted over the din of sixteen radios, two "tellys," a score of personal stereos and innumerable voices.

The man whom I had so recently mistaken for a waiter turned back to me.

"Whadda think we've just been discussin'?" he demanded in perfect Cockney.

"I missed the beginning," I explained, indicating my recorder. "Could you repeat it?"

A woman, dressed in gold and silver rings and pierced in places a gentleman doesn't describe in public, answered for her friend. From her I expected guttural street language and got, instead, Oxford English.

"It was a hit," she explained.

"A hit?"

"A direct hit."

"You mean, like a bomb?"

"Bombs are passé. No one uses bombs, anymore."

Remembering the money spent on *Star Wars, the Defense System,* I wished someone had told Ronald Reagan about that.

"So, what did they hit us with?"

"Auntie EM," she informed me with so bland an expression, I thought I was supposed to laugh.

"Auntie Em? Like in *The Wizard of Oz*?" While I wasn't a huge fan of that particular movie, I had seen it enough times to make a reasonable deduction that Auntie Em was no more dangerous than the mother on *The Waltons.* And I couldn't imagine how *she* could have knocked out a square mile of power.

"You livin' in a hole, man?"

"O.K." I conceded, attempting a wry smile. "Your world is in color and mine is in black and white. So elucidate me."

"Auntie EM," the young woman repeated as though she thought I was mentally deficient. "E.M. Electromagnetic fields." A flash bulb exploded over my head as I caught on.

That would have been enough, but unfortunately, I suffered from a problem common to most red-heads – I blush easily. The explanation and my subsequent comprehension of the young woman's explanation started the process, and once begun, no power on earth had proven effective in stopping it.

"Hey, man, look at him!" my helpful companion called to her friends. "He's turning red!"

"Someone call a fire truck!"   "When he gets ripe, pluck him," another of the group purred. Which did not help my condition.

Have I mentioned I also blush when I'm mad?

"O.K.," I said, backing away while holding up my hands, gangster victim-style. "Please tell me about – Auntie EM."

"Isn't he the polite one," another cooed, but this voice didn't make me blush, either from embarrassment or anger. Rather, it sent shivers of absolute dread down my spine. Standing on tiptoe (I'm not exactly short, but I'm no James Arness, either), I tried to put a face to the speaker. Unfortunately, there were so many young people gathered around me, I couldn't single him out.

I wanted to ask Joe Polite to step forward and I'd explain a thing or two about manners, but my words were drowned by a sea of others, all wishing to be helpful.

"Blowing people up is so crude," I was informed by lips whispering so close to my ear, my cartilage itched and my ear drum hummed. "It's messy."

"Yeah, well, it worked for your fathers," I stupidly protested. Even notice that when you're annoyed, you start defending points of view you'd never consider speaking up for when you're relaxed? Sort of like being drunk, except your excuse isn't as good.

"Bombs, guns, land mines; they're all weapons of the past."

"Well, there goes my stock in Gun Trafficking International," I sighed. "Shot to hell."

I guess I was funny and didn't know it, because they all laughed and slapped me on the back.

"That's right, man! You've got it!"

"Make love, not war," I added.

I guess I pushed my stand-up routine too far, for a well-orchestrated sigh escaped the crowd and several moved away. It was a crushing blow to my hopes for a career in the Catskills.

But at least I could breathe again.

"Come on, chaps," I pleaded, inadvertently stepping on someone's toes as I scrambled after one of the more talkative youths.

"Chums," he corrected me. "But who says we're your chums?"

"This does." I demonstrated my good will by holding up a ten pound note. I reasoned that if bombs and guns and land mines were passé, money was still a chum's best friend.

Guess what? I was right.

It was nice to know something from Past Civilizations still lived.

"Latte for the house," I called to the milktender behind the bar. Three cheers rang the rafters and I was back in their good graces as a "jolly olde fellow." Or something like that, I didn't quite catch.

"Tell me," I asked, holding my mini Radio Shack "spy" recorder out to the crowd, while being pushed into an empty chair. "About modern-day warfare."

A girl with a bald head and a snake tattooed around her temples pressed her face close to mine.

"It's the Age of Technology," she educated me. "No one wants to kill, anymore. I mean, if everyone's dead, who's going to do the menial labor?" I thought she was kidding, so I looked into her eyes, expecting to see bright, sparkling laughter in their depths.

When am I ever going to learn?

I nodded stiffly.

"Especially with health care costs so high," I guessed.

"It's a sin," she agreed.

"We're for peace," another chum informed me.

"But you approve of using technology to destroy people?"

"Not destroy; control."

"Tell me about it."

"Everything runs on power: computers, teles, motors."

"Watches," I added.

"Watches," my informant enthusiastically nodded. "What better way of fighting an enemy than by disabling his *toys?*"

"We're talking a little more than toys, here," I protested.

"They're things, man. You don't need *things* to live. We're for a cleaner way of life; a simpler way. Back to nature."

"Being simpler doesn't necessarily mean less expensive," I noted, my eyes glued to a green stone, d/b/a an emerald, suspended around his neck by a gold chain thick enough to have been a pit bull collar.

"This," he elucidated me, noting my interest, "is natural."

"No additives, no preservatives," I agreed, doing some mental arithmetic and deducing that emerald was probably worth the cumulative of more than three years of a reporter's salary. "Auntie EM," I tried again before I started crying. "How is it done?"

"No big deal," the girl with the snake scoffed. "Real simple."

"What does it take? An army with jamming devices?"

She looked at me as though *I* were the one with the shaved head and tattoo.

"We told you. No armies; no draft. No mess. A device like the one they used last night would have to be no bigger than a suitcase."

I was, in the vernacular of their ancestors, blown away.

"No bigger than a suitcase? Are you saying that the weapon which wiped out the power of one square mile was concealed in a tourist bag?"

"Not weapon. Device." I sat corrected. "That's what I said. But I didn't say it was brought in by a tourist."

"Who brought it in, then?"

"I didn't say it was 'brought in,' either."

"Who's-behind-it?"

She shrugged and flashed me a beautiful smile.

"How should I know?"

"You know everything else," I tried, appealing to her vanity.

"I don't really care. We all talk about it. It could have been any one of us. Electromagnetism is a fascinating subject."

"Yeah," I agreed, nodding my head in dumb stupefaction. "When I was a kid, we thought it was a big thrill to study positive and negative fields. You take two magnets," I demonstrated with two invisible, coin-sized magnets. "And move them toward one another. Likes attract, opposites repel. Pushing away one magnet without actually touching it with the other was a gas."

Everyone drew back from me as though they had been blown away by a sudden gush of wind. I guess they didn't understand my expression.

"It was fun," I hastened to correct. "Like magic. None of us ever thought of how to use it as a – device – for mass disruption."

"No," Joe Polite purred, nearly stopping my heart with the chill of his words. "They were too busy splitting atoms."

"Who said that?" I demanded, standing up and pushing away from the table. My reporter's instincts were working full blast. Someone in this group knew more about the practical application of EM than idle speculation.

And he was as dangerous as hell.

No one bothered to admit culpability. In fact, I guess they thought my sudden interest was funny, for they all sort of laughed at me.

"We're all one here," a voice from my right informed me.

"A family."

"Chums," I nodded, desperately searching the faces for one which looked off-kilter. Failing in that, I tried to memorize their features, engrave into my memory distinguishing marks I could call up later, if I ever saw one alone. In an alley. With a briefcase.

The problem was, they were all covered with distinguishing features: tattoos, spiked hair, shaved heads, colored spangles, six-inch fingernails, pointed eyebrows and rings of India brass pierced though every imaginable area of skin.

In a sea of differences, everyone looked the same.

Before I could mentally strip them of their costumes, someone sang out, "Look! There's Brittany!" and they turned, *en mass,* and rushed to the window. A moment later, my informants were gone, disappeared into the street, looking for "Brittany," whoever she was.

I slumped back into the chair, holding my head with my hands.

Not for the first time in my life I had found out more than I expected, and not nearly enough. It was disconcerting. A line of salty perspiration dribbled down my forehead.

"It is hot, isn't it?" the milktender agreed, incorrectly interpreting the cause of my sweat. "It's this global warming. We're killing the planet."

I got up and left, wondering if he had any idea how accurate his remark was.

A dire prediction having nothing whatsoever to do with the ozone hole.

What to do? If I were in Missouri, I'd pick up the phone and call Captain Helen Chandler of the St. Louis Police Department. She and I had had a perfect relationship. We got along like fire and water. But we respected one another's professionalism. I'd ask her if the department had received any bomb threats from some sort of splinter group and she'd tell me when there was information the Public needed to know, I'd be called.

And then she'd make some off-the-record remark about holding my breath....

In that way I'd have the information I was seeking. From the tone of her voice. If she sounded cranky and irritable, then I'd have confirmation. If she were light and breezy, I'd know she thought I was having fantasies.

This may sound like an odd way to communicate but it was better than some of the other relationships I've had with police personnel. Those usually went something like this:

"Hello, Captain/Lieutenant/Officer/Detective, this is Andy from CANS. (I hate to identify myself by saying, "This is Kimbo from CANS," because of the alliteration. It doesn't sound right, somehow.... Leads to images of Kimbo with a big "can".... and then we have a whole different kettle of fish, and I get thrown in the slammer for peddling – well, you know what.) "Has the department received any bomb threats –"

And then I'd be cut off with a string of expletives, universally ending with, "... and don't call me again. Ever!"

So you can see why I look back upon my association with Captain Chandler with emotions akin to tolerance.

I have only been in London several years, hardly long enough to have established any great animosities with the local authorities. I was optimistic that, given time, we would work it out to our mutual disadvantage, but at the moment no such intolerance existed.

That was enough of an excuse for me to give it the old college try. Stopping at a public phone booth, I dialed Scotland Yard.

"Hello," I tried in my most affable "I'm-on-your-side" voice. "My name is Andy Kimbo. I'm a reporter for the Carry-All News Service, investigating the power outage which occurred last night. I was wondering if Scotland Yard had received any warning calls about the incident."

"One moment, sir," a pleasant, officious voice advised me. "I will transfer you to the proper department."

"Tha—" which was all I got out of "thank you," before the line went dead.

Against my better judgment, and at the risk of spending my entire expense account for the month on Queen Bell, I called back.

"I was cut off before I could speak to someone about the power outage last night –"

"One moment, sir," a different, equally pleasant voice informed me.

This time I didn't bother to say "thank you," as the familiar dead-line humming filled my ear.

This was getting me nowhere fast. But the familiar feelings of *deja vu* did warm the cockles of my heart.

As much as things change, they always stay the same.

Changing phones, in case they had traced the call and could nail my name to a specific pay phone number, I called back. This time I tried a different, albeit slightly illegal, tract.

"I wanna speak to someone aboot that warnin' we give you blokes last night," I demanded. "Unless you want it to happen ag'in, you'd better –"

"What's your code word?" the suddenly not-so-pleasant voice demanded. I could see I had hit a nerve.

I thought fast.

"Auntie EM," I fed him.

After a series of hums, clicks and buzzes not calculated to steady the nerves, another voice came on the line.

"This is Rocket Scientist," I was informed. "What have you got for me?"

My mouth went dry. I felt as though I were Ming the Merciless about to inform Flash Gordon of my plans to destroy the earth.

"About last night," I began. When my voice failed, I cleared my throat and tried again. "I want to talk to you about electromagnetic fields."

"This isn't Auntie EM. Who are you?" the Voice On The Other End demanded with less than civil politeness.

Would you think less of me if I told you my sphincter tightened to prevent a sudden accident, as my bowels turned against me?

"Sorry. Wrong number."

I hung up the telephone and started to bolt, when early training took hold of me and shook my consciousness until my teeth rattled. Taking my handy-handy, all-purpose handkerchief from my back pocket, I wiped all incriminating fingerprints from the handset and the numbered push buttons, then took off like a cat whose tail had just been trodden on.

It didn't take a rocket scientist to deduce I had hit onto the correct code name or that I had plummeted myself into the bowels of a Scotland Yard investigation. Assuming our brief conversation had been recorded and was, at this very moment, being put through the spin cycle of a voice analyzer, I was now a marked man.

An inadvertent charter member of the Auntie EM fan club. Only the cops wouldn't be looking me up for an autograph; they'd be reserving a cell for me in solitary confinement.

All because I was just trying to do my job.

I was, after all, an investigative reporter.

"How many times have I told you, Kimbo, the first two letters of 'investigative reporter' should stand for 'responsible'?" Sweet demanded, spittle flying from his lips. "If Scotland Yard told you there was nothing to the power outage last night, then there's nothing to it. Understand? That's plain, good old American English!"

"But this is England," I complained. "They don't speak good old American English here. They use good olde Double-Speak."

He rolled his eyes. He was very good at that, by the way. It was his trademark. If he were an actor, I could have compared the gesture to Zasu Pits, wringing her hands.

I had just returned from a police 'intelligence-parting session,' where, in the great tradition of law enforcement agencies everywhere, they had managed to impart no new information over the course of an excruciatingly long forty-five minute briefing.

Giving an entirely new meaning to the word "brief."

"I don't want any trouble," Sweet was saying. "We don't want to make enemies of the authorities. It would not be overestimating to say our very existence as a news gathering organization depends upon the good will of Scotland Yard."

I knew all about Good Will; I had gotten many a shirt and pair or trousers from them during my days as an itinerant. In that line of charity, they did good work. I knew of no other "good will" which served the public.

"But Sweet, they came out and said there's nothing to last night's incident. That was a bald-faced lie."

"Andy, why are you always so suspicious?"

"Occupational hazard," I grinned. He failed to see the charm I injected into that patented facial expression.

"If the local authorities say there's nothing to it, why do you always think you know better?"

How could I tell him my sources were a bunch of alien-looking chums from a coffee *haus*? How explain to Mister Bottom Line that bombs were passé and all the new weapons were carried by innocuous-looking tourists with T-shirts reading, "Nessie Lives"?

"I heard, by the way," he added, "that you minded your P's and Q's at the press briefing. Never said a word. I'm proud of you."

Whenever Sweet was proud of me, it was always for the wrong reasons.

"Yes, sir. Thank you, sir."

You're damned right I was silent. Until I put a face to "Rocket Scientist," I didn't want anybody hearing my voice. The sound of a cell door slamming shut was just too vivid.

And then it hit me.

"Who said I didn't say a word?" I demanded.

"You're not the only one with contacts." His chest puffed out like the Marlboro Man. "Unlike you, I have always made it a policy to get along with my fellow news gathering associates. One of them called me after the briefing."

"You were checking upon me?"

"Now don't look at it that way," he soothed in that fatherly voice which always spelled trouble. "Let's just say, I'm keeping an eye on all of you."

"You're not my guardian, for God's sake!" I protested.

"Guardian. Yes," he slowly replied, stroking his chin. "If you don't toe the line here, I suppose there *are* other papers you could work for. *Not,"* he added with a grin.

That was Sweet's attempt at a joke.

We in the news gathering business are not known for our wit.

If we were, we'd anchor the ten o'clock news and make a heck of a lot more money.

People would even respect us. It's not easy reading from a prompter what other people have written.

"I'm not going to write a fluff piece about brown- and blackouts," I stubbornly protested.

"There's always that article on Princes Di's death," he reminded me.

I slunk away with my tail tucked twixt my legs.

ACT 5

"Gypsy," I grumbled, forking around the last noodle on the plate with so vicious a gyration, I made myself seasick. "I am *not* going to write this up as just another electrical overload. You and I both know it's far more insidious than that."

She sadly shook her head. She did it so often I assumed it was a hereditary trait.

"I think you ought to write it, exactly as Mr. McGraw suggested."

My head shot up so fast you'd think some invisible puppet master had it on a string.

"He called you," I accused. "Gave you some bull about my following orders; crapped about the good of the news service; harped on how important it is to keep on 'sterling' terms with Scotland Yard."

Her eyes opened wide and she leaned across the table, a picture of wonder.

"Bull?" she asked. "Crapped? Harped? That last I know; it is a musical instrument, consisting of a triangular frame set with strings and plucked by the fingers. Shall I play one for you?"

"You play the harp?"

"Certainly. And I am glad to see Mr. McGraw plays, also."

"The only thing Sweet plays is the horses," I bitched. Strike that. ~~Bitched.~~ Poor word choice. Correct to, "The only thing Sweet plays is the horses," I *complained.*

(Writers are always editing their own work, even if they're just thinking in their minds. I didn't want to have to explain the Americanization of a female dog in heat to Gypsy.)

"You are not being fair," she pursued. "I have heard him sing; he had a beautiful voice. Also, he plays violin and piano. I have seen the baby grand in his flat."

"Harp," I explained, "means to lecture. When I say Sweet harped on keeping on good terms with Scotland Yard, I mean, he went on and on and on about it. The other words mean approximately the same thing. Crapped means to bitc – complain – in a nagging voice."

"I see," she brightened. "When he plays the horses, he bets on nags!"

"No!" I shouted. "To nag means to pester."

"And to crap means –"

I threw up my hands in despair.

"Oh, shit!"

She was one step ahead of me.

"Exactly!"

"I dropped my head down onto the plate, indenting it with the impression of a noodle.

Which some people might say, is a good trick.

"Gypsy, you shouldn't believe everything Sweet says. He's only an editor. Not God. He makes suggestions, gives advice... like a lovelorn columnist," I faltered.

"You mean, I should not believe him when he said to tell you to pick up your paycheck at the office?"

"What?"

"He called to leave you a message. Today is payday. You went away without picking up your check." And then pitifully, "You have not gotten paid?" And then more cheerfully, "No matter. You are staying with me; we are 'roomies,' are we not? We share expenses. When you do not have any money I will support you –"

"Wait a minute! You mean, Sweet *didn't* call to give you some song and dance about asking me to write an article on a blackout, instead of my doing some snooping to discover what this electromagnetic field threat is all about?"

"No song. No dance," she agreed. "He spoke in his normal voice. And I could not have seen him dance over the phone," she reminded me. "Although it is a lovely thought. Do you like to dance?"

"I never learned," I pouted.

"I will teach you –"

"Gypsy," I exploded. "If Sweet didn't tell you to influence me, why do you want me to write a story about a blackout?"

She smiled.

"I like to see your name in print. A by-line. It makes me very proud. Also, it is a good idea to go on record as stating your belief the power outage was no more than a routine occurrence. 'Happens all the time; a disease of modern civilization.' That will make Rocket Scientist and Auntie EM very happy. They will cross your name off their lists of suspicious characters."

The tortoise finally caught the hare.

"Now, I get it! You want me to throw them off my track by writing some –"

"Crap," she filled in the blank.

I threw my arms around her and squeezed her until her face turned red. It was only after we looked like twins (she by the blood pooling to her face, I by heredity) that I released her.

"Gyp! Great idea."

"More prudent than great," she admitted. "But it is nice to know we are both on the same wave length. Go into the living room and type your story while I make coffee. Then we can relax and play a game."

"What game?" I suggestively inquired.

"Anything you like." Before I could undress the photographic image of the game I wanted to play, her eyes brightened. "Monopoly. I have a board."

"Oh, joy."

As an incentive to go to work, it worked like a charm.

By the time she had the coffee prepared, I has well into my article.

"Listen to this," I read as she poured pressed java into small, half-melon shaped, clear glass cups. "The setting: downtown London. The scene: small businesses, residential suites. The time: Midnight. The action: Blackout. The cast: hundreds of people, milling about. A new theatrical production rehearsing for its debut on Theatre Row? Tourists lining up for a tour through Buckingham Palace? A 12:00

A.M. sale at Harrods? Fans from two local Cricket Clubs behaving in perfectly acceptable bedlam?

"Wrong on all counts. Londoners were subjected to a total power outage, effecting everything from blenders to cellular phones –"

"We call them 'mobiles,'" she corrected me.

I typed out my mistake without losing a beat.

"The dreaded Curse of Civilization had struck, without so much as a 'by your leave.' Spokesmen for Queen Electric were quick to fix the blame on an overuse of air conditioning, while an unidentified source at the Ministry protested that the unusually high demand for electrical energy was due to the fact local bartenders refused to draw ale according to EU standards, issuing cold, frosty ones in outdated pint glasses."

"Vivid," she approved. "You have said nothing in a clever way, wasting exactly one hundred and forty-eight words."

"Thank you. Whoever said a liberal education was wasted on the masses?"

I picked up my cup, observing as I did so, a very neat depiction of the world etched on the outside. I positively beamed. (Not *up,* Scotty, thank you. For the moment, I was happy where I was.)

"Nescafe!" I observed, reading the raised lettering on the bottom of the cup. "I have a set exactly like this. How did you get them?"

"The same way you did. I saved inner seal foils. When I had enough, I mailed them in with my check to cover postage and handling."

"Gypsies respond to advertising, just like the rest of us?"

She nodded.

"I also got a troll through the post by saving the wrappers of taffy."

Was it any wonder why I loved this woman?

"But," I held her at bay by waving a finger in the air. "Do you have drinking glasses with Tom and Jerry on them?"

She looked sad.

"No. But I have a Cadbury tin in the shape of an old fashioned telephone booth. Will that do?"

I considered.

"Only if you keep pennies or rubber bands in it."

I could she her mind working.

"It is filled with plastic worms and bugs which glow in the dark," she remembered.

I was so excited I spilled my coffee. She was prepared for such a contingency, passing me a red and white checkered towel to absorb that which my pants had not.

"Finish writing while I set up the Monopoly game."

It didn't take long to fill two pages with utter nonsense, uninformed quotes and idle speculation. I did not fail to mention the prediction I had overheard on the street that it was most certainly, "the end of the world."

Editors and newswire subscribers just loved comments from the Idiot in the Street.

When I finished, I positioned myself in front of the game. We rolled the dice to see who would go first. I won. Shaking them a second time, I blew into my cupped hand for luck, then rolled a five and a three. Blithely marching my Scottie dog down the requisite number of squares, I stopped on the appropriate square. As any aficionado knows, eight squares down the first row lands you on Vermont Avenue.

"I'll buy it for $100," I remarked. It was only then I realized something was terribly amiss. I was not on Vermont, and the price was not $100. I squinted, leaned forward, frowned, pursed my lips then held out a limp hand, palm upturned.

"That's not Vermont," I protested. "It's —" But I could not read the name without putting on my reading glasses. I fumbled for them, held them up without actually putting them on (wearing reading glasses is a sign of age) and pouted.

"Euston Road? What the hell is a Euston Road? There isn't anything like that on the Monopoly board."

I looked around the room for incriminating briefcases, filled with space-altering equipment.

Gypsy appeared surprised.

"It is as it has always been."

"Vermont is supposed to be there," I pursued.

Gypsy inspected the board. Apparently some alien had taken over her body, for she adamantly disagreed with me.

"This is correct," she asserted.

"No, it's not. Look; I can play this game in my sleep. The first row is Mediterranean, Community Chest, Baltic, Income Tax, Reading Railroad (pronounced the good ol' USA way as, "Look at Johnny read!"), Oriental, Chance, Vermont, Connecticut and Jail. This is – some sort of perverted Monopoly!"

"It is English Monopoly," she sniffed. "You are in England, now."

"I may be in England, but there are certain constants in life."

"Like death and taxes," she supplied. I nodded agreement.

"Like Golden Arches signifying hamburgers and Vermont being three squares past the railroad on the Monopoly board. And what's this?" I demanded, holding up the paper money. Rather that the pleasing little blue fifties, yellow tens and pink fives with their familiar, comforting, dollar signs, what I was clutching was not only incorrectly color-coded, but had cursive "L's" with equal signs through them printed on the backs.

"Pounds, sterling," Gypsy supplied.

"My God!" I screamed. "Pink 500's? Orange one hundreds; white fifties? Sacrilegious!"

"It looks right to me."

"No, no, this is all wrong," I protested, feeling disoriented. While I've never considered myself an American snob, some things are decidedly untouchable.

"You are then, a literalist?" she asked.

I faltered, shook my head, then rolled my eyes as visions of Supreme Court arguments and catfights over differences in Aramaic, Greek and Latin filled my mind.

Gypsy picked the dice up off the board and rolled.

Five; a three and a two. She moved to – gasp – Kings Cross Station (British Railways). The cost was two hundred pounds. She plunked down two orange bills, took her deed and nodded toward me.

I rolled doubles, two's.

Marching like a Politically Incorrect Boy Scout, I landed on – the Electric Company.

It was Fate.

When everything else was totally messed up, there was the good olde Electric Company.

As much as things change, they remain the same.

A shiver ran down my spine. I suspected I had been EM'd.

"Are you going to buy it?" Gypsy inquired.

I had a feeling I had *already* bought it.

Along with the Farm.

We played for an hour, but it just wasn't the same. I mean, how can Piccadilly relate to Pacific Avenue, or Mayfair compare to Boardwalk? And who ever heard of taking a chance and receiving the direction, "Advance to Trafalgar Square. If you pass 'Go' collect 200 pounds"?

I lost handily. My heart just wasn't in it. It was pitiful.

"Want to play a different game?" Gypsy asked as she put the pieces away. I shook my head.

"I don't think I could bear another shock."

Imagine playing poker, where the Kings have names of Edward, Henry, John and Richard instead of suites like clubs and diamonds, and where the joker's face resembled the Prince of Wales?

I went back to writing my story. It wasn't easy keeping references to Evil Empires out of the text. When I was through, I proofed it (no one should ever spell-check their own writing) and tapped the pages neatly together so they were all the same height.

"Wait up for me while I run this over to the office?" I asked.

She agreeably nodded.

"I have some work to do, myself. I have a client coming in the morning who has many questions which require an answer."

"Like what?" I asked, digging for my keys.

"Do you wish me to divulge privileged information?"

I stopped, hand still in my pocket.

"You mean psychics hold answers confidential, like shrinks and lawyers?"

"Most people who consult me would not like their private affairs revealed."

"I don't know," I shrugged, extracting my key ring. Aside from numerous keys to apartments I no longer rented, I had on my chain a pocket flashlight, pen knife, a duplicate to the engine and door keys to my Chevy Monza I had left in St. Louis, the one-key-opens-all for my Czech Republic, hamster-driven Roadster, and a plastic medallion with the image of a Cardinal and the numbers, 3,000,000 imprinted under it.

Anyone who knows anything about "baseball the way it outta be," knows that was a free token given to every adult fan with a paid admission after the Great White Rat's team broke the attendance record at Busch Stadium.

That was before the National League started counting tickets sold, rather than bodies through the turnstiles, American League style. It used to be "no show, no count." Now they add pigeons flying overhead to the totals and make three million every year.

It sure makes baseball sound like the great American game, but birds don't buy brew and they don't pay for parking, either.

Waving Gypsy good-bye, I trotted out, hopped down the stairs and scurried for my car. The off-street parking (there are no such things as apartment parking garages, or driveways in G.B.) was only sixteen blocks away, so I reached my motor in good time. It was only when I was half way to work that a bolt of lightning, far greater than any carried in a briefcase, struck me.

"What do you mean, you saw a baby grand in his flat?" I shrieked to thin air.

I didn't have to be psychic to hear Gypsy's laughter.

ACT 6

The story ran, newspapers bought it and Sweet was happy. Deliriously happy. When he saw me next morning, he slapped me on the back and offered to buy me coffee.

"No thanks," I demurred.

"Why not?"

He sounded hurt.

"Because I don't think I deserve it."

"It was a great story; it sold like hotcakes. What's not to like?"

"There wasn't a word of truth in it."

I could see the "So what?" forming on hip lips, but he bit it off.

"What do you mean, there wasn't a word of truth in it? You reported exactly what Scotland Yard said; in a clever and original way," he added, seeing the expression on my face.

"Don't try and soft soap me. I'm an ash-and-lye man. I want it straight, no frills."

"I thought you did an excellent job writing up a routine news story. You put *savoir faire* into it. A lot of people got excited over nothing. Granted, they were inconvenienced, but that's modern civilization. You said so yourself. So, you covered the angles and incidentally happened to draw the same conclusions as the authorities. I don't see anything iniquitous with that. They can't be wrong all the time, you know."

Had he meant it as a joke I would have laughed.

And meant it.

"Sweet, will you shut up and listen to me?"

His eyes narrowed and he stepped back, as though suddenly realizing I was covered with highly contagious poison ivy. (Which doesn't grow in the British Isles, which is something in its favor. Just like they don't have snakes in Ireland, but that isn't true and no poison ivy is.)

"Why is it I hear warning bells whenever you say that?"

"Because you're still a reporter at heart, Sweet. It's your news sense stirring your blood. You have an inkling –"

"– that I'm not going to like what you're going to say."

Grabbing me by my ear, a bad habit he developed several years ago when trying to prove I was a loud-mouthed, immature "boy," he dragged me into his office and shut the door.

"Whatever it is you're going to say, I don't want *them* to hear it," he warned. By "them," he meant my fellow news-gathering peers. It wasn't for my benefit that he sought solitude; he was afraid one of them would rat on him to The Old Man that he was being manipulated by A. Kimbo.

I really wasn't trying to do that, but I suppose it might look that way to interested observers.

"All right." he sighed. "Let me have it. Short and sweet."

I could hear Gypsy now:

"But Mr. McGraw, you are not short –"

I smiled and he took offense.

"Spit it out before I clam you up for good."

Which meant I had his ear. It was like that between us. When we talked as though we were gumshoes out of the '40's working on some sleazy caper, I knew I was "in."

"I want you to let me nose around, see what I can dig up. That wasn't some innocuous power outage. Someone perpetrated it. It was a test; a trial run, if you like." I could see he didn't "like," so I hurried on. "It's modern warfare, Sweet. How much do you think the government would pay someone threatening to knock out all the power in a hundred mile radius? A thousand mile radius?"

"You think some nutty group is blackmailing England?"

"I don't think they're nutty. I think they're dangerous. Maybe murderous."

"Who would do such a thing?"

"That's what I want to find out."

"But Scotland Yard said –"

"I know what Scotland Yard said. But listen." I lowered my voice conspiratorially, forcing him to bend forward. "On a hunch, I called and pretended to be a spokesman for this group – whomsoever they are. I used the name I heard at that coffee *haus* – never mind what," I hastened to add before he asked. I didn't want him to know. A little knowledge, as they say, is dangerous.

"So?"

"I hit pay dirt. I said I wanted to give a warning and got right to Scotland Yard's top man. I didn't get past him, but I *did* prove that there are a lot of people taking this very seriously."

He slowly nodded, then turned his back on me and walked to the window. I started a slow count to ten. Before I reached the half way point, Sweet took a pen out of his breast pocket and started poking around in his ear for some elusive ear wax.

"Has it ever occurred to you that if Scotland Yard is taking this seriously, perhaps we ought to let them handle it?"

"No."

He turned back to face me, wiping the end of his pen on the inside of his left sleeve.

"Why not?"

It was the classic, "Why do you think you'll have better luck than trained professionals?"

"Because I can go places they can't. Do things they can't."

"Illegal things?"

That was the *coup de gras.*

"That's why we have laws, Andy. To protect people from unwarranted intrusions, police brutality. Search warrants; Miranda. Court orders. By putting yourself outside the law, you become a renegade. Crooks have rights, too."

"I just want permission to sniff around. Ask questions. Listen to answers. Get a feel for the discontent in *circulation.*"

That last, being a newspaper term, really got to him. How could an editor turn his nose up at anything having to do with circulation?

It was worse than hanging up the phone on a potential subscriber.

As anyone who's ever watched a TV series knows, it's the ratings which count, not the quality of the programming.

"You just want to nose around? No more?"

"No more."

"You won't go joining any of these fringe outfits, just to get a story?"

"Who, me?"

"You won't go getting yourself killed?"

I started to say, "I'll try not to," then changed my tune.

"Certainly not!"

"And you'll share whatever you get with the proper authorities?"

"Once the story is in the can."

It was a mixed metaphor; stories go out on the wire; films go in the can. I knew once he figured it out he'd know I had my head on straight.

"And you won't ask for a big expense account? Something roughly equal to the gross national product of Paraguay?"

Since neither of us had a clue what that was, I felt safe in agreeing.

"All right. Take the rest of the week. See what you come up with. But, I want you to report to me on a daily basis. And wear your beeper."

"I will," I agreed, nodding like Garfield in a car window.

"Then get out of here. And don't say I didn't warn you. If I get one hint of trouble – one call from Scotland Yard that you're hindering their investigation – one 3 A.M. summons to come and bail you out – that's it! Got it?"

"Yes, sir."

"Don't 'yes, sir' me. That always means you're not listening."

"I'm listening," I swore, my mind already out the door.

"And don't say you're listening. That means you think I've given you a license to do whatever you damned well please. And that I'll back you to the hilt. I won't. Are you following me?"

"Right on."

He threw up his hands in despair.

"Get out. And for God's sake –"

"Watch my P's and Q's," I finished.

"Shut the door behind you," he overlapped.

I'd done a better snow job that I thought.

I returned to *La Boutique,* the coffee haus I had inadvertently discovered the morning after the EM attack. My intention was to interview some of the patrons in the hope of putting a face to Joe Polite. To my disappointment, the place was almost empty.

"Where'd everybody go?" I asked the milktender, sidling up to the bar. His answer came by way of a raised eyebrow. "Your customers?" I added. "The music too low?" I noted the modern-day version of the juke box was turned way down, and that there were no musicians playing discordant tunes to contrast the canned variety.

"They migrated," he replied.

I glanced outside to see whether the seasons had changed and no one told me.

"It certainly couldn't be that advertisement" (pronounced ad-*verd*-ess-ment by the locals), I prodded, indicating a gaudy sign in the window I was reading backwards. When the disinterested employee didn't reply, I got up and walked to the front. Taking the professionally printed ad down, I turned it around and read the printing out loud.

"Frenchmen: *Attention!* Reproduction is Your Responsibility, too! Do not be held captive by outdated Napoleonic Laws! If the French Government forbids your *Self-Mutilation* by Vasectomy, get the Simply Painless, Inexpensive Operation in London! Make it a part of your Weekend Visit!" And then, in a smaller point size, "Consultation with an Experienced Physician, surgery and out-patient recovery all within the hour. Arrive in England a fertile, baby-making machine, leave for Home a Safe and Happy (and sterile) Romeo!

"No more worries about unwanted pregnancies or entangling alliances! Sew your Wild Oats without Worries over paternity suits!

Bring home your Certificate and see what a difference it makes in your marriage! Your wife will love you as she never has before!"

I don't know what shocked me more: the text, the implicit promises, or the misuse of the word "sew."

However, on a scale of 1 to 10, it sure was an attention getter.

Remember that '60's song, sung by Jay and the Americans, "Only in America"? (Chant it to yourself: Only in A-mer-a-ca...) You know the one – written for The Drifters, but the Powers-That-Be thought it inappropriate for a black group to sing? Well, I guess the lyrics could be updated to, "Only in En-ga-la-nd."

Pretty scary.

Replacing the sign, I returned to the milktender.

"What's your name?" I asked, more for the sake of making conversation than from any personal or professional interest.

He muttered something unintelligible, then asked, in perfect Queen's English, "What's yours?"

"Sorry, I didn't catch it," I grinned, suddenly realizing I did not want to give anyone near the scene of the crime my name.

"Wshfderes," he replied. "What's yours?"

"Kertbny," I affably answered. Which is sort of like, "@#*&^%$(*!!" but using letters rather than symbols.

"I saw you in here the other day, didn't I?" he asked.

"Yeah," I agreed. "I was the guy who ordered a short one, twist of lime, drop of lemon, hold the ice. Stirred anti-clockwise," I added. I could have said, "Shaken, not stirred," but didn't want to sound like the spy I suddenly felt transformed into.

"We don't sell alcohol here."

"Oh. You must be remembering some other chapstick," I retorted in my best Americanese.

The milktender shrugged and wiped the counter. I had seen that gesture in lots of TV Westerns. It was a signal to the Outlaws that the Lawman had just walked in.

"Be seeing you," I waved, giving him the "OK" sign with thumb and forefinger, then hurrying out before a huge balloon could come out of the back room and chase me down the street.

I hadn't discovered Joe Polite but I had convinced myself that cafe knew more than it was saying.

I wandered in and out of several other milk bars and coffee shoppes, nosing around for any of the same crowd I had seen at *La Boutique,* but I didn't get very far. Most of them were filled with tourists disguised as MPs, and natives looking, for all the world, like normal, everyday working stiffs, grabbing a Danish before clocking in at Kellogg's.

There wasn't much else I could do prospectively, so I decided to do some checking retrospectively. Reasoning that if Scotland Yard already had a Rocket Scientist in place to receive phone warnings, they had been onto Auntie EM for some time, I decided to play catch up. Maybe this past incident hadn't been the first of many EM attacks; maybe it was the second or third, each one a little bigger, a little more threatening.

Where else to go but into the recesses of journalistic past?

And who better to take with me on my journey down Memory Lane than a Gypsy?

Hoping into my Roadster (has anyone seriously used that word since the Nancy Drew Mysteries popularized it?), I drove over to Gypsy's place of work and knocked on the door. After a moment, I heard a familiar, welcoming "Hello!"

Opening the door, I was immediately assailed by the smell of burning incense. Hooking fingers over my nose, clothespin style, I waved with my other hand and attempted to back out. She hurried to me.

"I say hello, you say good-bye?" she quoted questioningly.

Still holding my nose, I replied, my voice sounding disguised because of it.

"I don't want to bother you when you're working."

"My client has just left," she assured me. "Did you not see the long line of black limousines driving away?"

"Nancy Reagan paid you a visit?" I gasped. "What did she want to know – what day to have her hair done?"

"That is unfair, Kimbo," Gypsy retorted, ushering me in.

"Maybe," I reluctantly agreed. "But responsible people don't go to mystics for advice on how to arrange travel schedules for the President of the United States. And, he stole the election from Jimmy Carter."

"Do many people think so?"

"I don't care if no people think so. I think so. The entire hostage crisis was manipulated to make Jimmy appear weak. Which he isn't."

She nodded wisely, while I went and opened a window.

"One day, your President Carter is going to win the Nobel Peace Prize."

I tingled in anticipation. I don't "trade" things often but if given a choice between Jimmy Carter winning the Nobel Peace prize and my winning a Pulitzer, I would give him first dibs. He isn't perfect but he's a man of courage and he cares about truth. Not many before or since can claim that distinction.

I blew my nose before coming back to the present.

"What do people see in incense? It makes my nose run and my eyes water."

"You would be a poor candidate for aroma therapy," she laughed. "Unless I used essence of coffee, mixed, perhaps with a subtle flavoring of vanilla."

My goose bumps turned to cold sweat as I made the connection with Captain Chandler. On Gypsy's approval I sent her vanilla-scented lotion as a means of congratulating her on her promotion from lieutenant. It had mixed results.

"That's the ticket," I agreed. "But you didn't answer my question. What do people see in incense?"

"I do not know that they 'see' anything," she chuckled.

"They use incense in church on holy days," I pursued.

"And do you know why?"

"I sure as hell do. It's pagan. Mysterious. It conjures up mental images of ghosts hovering behind half-obscured statues, ancient Druid worship, harvest celebrations, black candles and Powers From Beyond."

"Then," she sighed, "I suppose I ought not to use it."

"Why not?" I complained, having talked myself into the promotion of incense.

"I have no statues."

"None?" I asked, clearly surprised. "No dying Gauls, no nostalgic images of Gypsies on horseback, stealing children?"

Gypsy rolled her eyes.

"You watch too much late-night television." No argument there. "One day I will take you to a Gypsy encampment and show you what their life is truly like."

"They depict Gypsies in numerous old black and white horror movies. Very colorful characters. Do you remember the scene from *House of Frankenstein,* where a very young Elena Verdugo dances for Lon Chaney, Jr.? That actress was actually a descendent of wealthy Spaniards, you know. Her family was still in possession of a land grant from the king of Spain, covering much of Los Angeles, including the entire area where Universal Studios was constructed."

"Which impressed you more?" she teased. "Her dancing, her distant relations, or the fact she might have become the new landlord of a movie lot?"

That was a hard question, put to a boy who appreciated high art, and who also had aspirations of becoming a famous screenwriter in another, if not this lifetime.

"Want to go to the morgue?" I answered, instead.

"Are you feeling ill?"

"I think I'll be all right once I breathe some fresh air."

"We are leaving London?"

"No," I naively replied.

"Are we going to visit a friend of yours? Hold a séance?"

I was, proverbially, hit by a ton of bricks.

"No, no," I reassured her. Her face fell. "Not morgue, as in dead people; morgue, as in dead news."

"We are going to relive Yesteryear with the Lone Ranger?"

It spoke well of her background. We had much in common.

"We're going to do a background check on power outages. I want to know if this last EM attack was the first or just the biggest. If there were others we can tie Auntie to, we can establish a pattern; maybe even predict where and when she'll strike again."

"To what end?"

"Stopping whomever is perpetrating these evil deeds."

"Clayton Moore would approve. I am ready."

She and I scurried out the door. It shut behind us but I didn't hear it lock. When I pointed this fact out to her, Gypsy smiled. Her grin bore a distinct resemblance to Bela Lugosi's Igor contemplating mayhem. It bode well for our enterprise.

There's something about the musty old smell of newsprint and reading half-smudged, curling, yellowed paper which stirs the blood. Of course, we weren't investigating ancient stories, such as the allegation Sir Arthur Conan Doyle stole the plot for "The Hound of the Baskervilles," then murdered his best friend so he could continue his liaison with the dead man's wife, so the newspapers we perused weren't that old.

Call it nostalgia.

There's also no place on earth quite so romantic as a newspaper archive. There, amid the thoughts and deeds of days gone by, I could stand, shoulder-to-shoulder with the woman I cared deeply about, and soak in the essence of her active, inquiring mind.

Who could ask for more?

We morgue hopped, going from one newspaper archive to the next, in glorious isolation. I took notes on my legal-sized yellow tablet and my cheap Mercantile Bank pen, while Gypsy turned the pages of the newspapers, occasionally pausing to wipe her ink-stained hands on a ratty Kleenex.

We decided to go back one year, then work our way forward. With all of Great Britain to investigate, we finally decided to narrow our search to England. Our reasoning was simple: Ireland already had its own war, Scotland wasn't exciting enough for terrorists to bother with, and if Wales had power outages, no one would consider it worth reporting.

"Look!" Gypsy exclaimed, pointing to a small blurb buried on page ten of the *Times.* I looked.

The story, headlined in twelve-point to underscore its relative unimportance, read: "Local school loses power. Students sent home." The article noted that a local grammar school had lost electrical power, shutting down all lights in the building and affecting everything run on batteries. The heating system was also disrupted. Because outside temperatures hovered at the 40 degree mark, the principal dismissed classes. An aside mentioned that all term exams would be cancelled. No cause for the power outage had been isolated.

"How convenient," I sagely observed, rubbing my hands together in empathy with the disappointed students. "It sounds as if someone didn't want to take a test."

"Or perhaps were subjecting the teachers to a test they did not know they were taking," Gypsy added.

I turned to see if she were reading my mind, then realized, foolishly, that few people outside educational circles failed to identify with a class of kids receiving an unexpected reprieve from a dreaded examination.

I set the paper aside, intending to have the article Xeroxed when we were through, when Gypsy stopped me with a shake of her head. (Note, I used a capital "X." Although the word has been adopted into popular usage, it still reflects a brand name.)

"Perhaps I am – paranoid? But I think it best we just extract the details from the report without asking to have it copied."

"Yeah. You could be right," I agreed. "Who knows? One of the students from that school may be working here part-time. Even with today's low educational standards, a relatively bright person would be able to deduce the object of our search, if we hand them six or seven stories on power outages."

"When we go to interview the principal, I do not suggest you mention that opinion."

I sighed and nodded agreement. While it's a commonly held belief each generation thinks those who come after them have it easy in school and graduate nearly illiterate, it was closer to a Truism than an Old Wives Tale.

"An Old *Husband's* Tale," Gypsy corrected me.

"What?"

"I do not like expressions which denigrate women," she explained. *"He runs like a pregnant woman; She is a blonde bubblehead; She's as plain as an Old Maid.* I prefer, *he runs like an Old Man with an enlarged prostate.* And why should blonde women be the standard by which bubbleheads are judged? I have seen just as many stupid blond men. And why should an unmarried woman be called an 'Old Maid,' when a unattached man has the dignity of being called a bachelor?"

"You're right," I admitted. "That's the problem with language."

"How is it you would say?" She thought a minute and came up with a Kimboism. "'The winners write the history about the losers.' Is that not it? And as males do most of the talking, they create the expressions which form the basis of our idiomatic phrases."

"That's it. But you had better be careful to whom you say such things. If McGraw hears that from your lips, he'll think I've contaminated you."

"Oh," she laughed, dismissing the idea. "He thinks that already."

We went back to work.

Exactly a month after the date of the school power failure we found another article, this one longer and more detailed, in that it dealt with money. It seems there was a blackout on Theatre Row, affecting all the major playhouses. Exactly at curtain time, the electricity went out, forcing 'controlled evacuations,' and 'a refund of ticket prices,' costing producers thousands of pounds in lost revenue.

"Now that I read this, I remember the incident. Aside from being glad I wasn't there, I passed it off as being –"

"The Curse of Modern Civilization," she filled in for me.

"Right. The power goes out and no one really thinks anything about it. We grumble, shrug our shoulders and wait for the Powers That Be to restore what is no longer a convenience but a necessity. As long as we don't have to wait too long, it's no big deal.

"And all the while, these innocuous little incidents are piling up. A school loses heat and lights; a group of theatre operators have to refund tickets; residents of some high-priced dwellings have their late night telly cut off. No big deal. No one sees the larger picture because we're all used to such things. The thought of a conspiracy never occurs to us.

"But if these incidents are not isolated – if they are, in fact, the testing grounds for some disenfranchised 'Back to Basics' group – we could wake up one morning to discover the toaster won't pop with our breakfast bread, the newspaper hadn't been delivered and all the military instillations are out of business."

"Make Love, not War," Gypsy happily chirped, which made me take a second look at her.

"You sure you're not in on this?" I demanded, only half kidding.

"Oh, how could I be? How would I operate my levitating table, or run the sound system which plays Uncle Harry's voice from Beyond?"

Which fell about a kilometer short of reassuring me.

ACT 7

"What does a school, a row of theatres and a city block have in common?" I asked out loud, although I could have saved myself the trouble. Gypsy was not only good at readings minds, she was a psychic. Better even than Claire Bloom, from "The Haunting." Her character, Theo, was a legend at Yale, having correctly identified 19 out of 20 playing cards held out, backs to her.

I'm not exactly a movie buff but I have been known to spend many sleepless nights in front of the Modern Day babysitter.

Gypsy chose to answer my musings rather than the stated question.

"It was Duke, not Yale."

"Are you sure?" I asked with a frown, before realizing what she had done, compelling me to do a 180. "I thought you promised not to read my mind!"

"Yes," she admitted with a smile which might have done good service on the face of the Gerber trademark. "It was the Psychic Lab at Duke University."

"How do you know? I didn't think Gypsy caravans were connected to electricity."

"I raised my antennae and brought in the signals through a Yuglosivian television station," she stated with such verity I came close to believing her.

She laughed at my pout.

"They are not major areas of import."

"What?" I asked, lost between Ivy League schools and Martians.

"A school, places of entertainment, residences and small businesses; they are not strategic locations. If someone were to adversely affect the power at Scotland Yard or 10 Downing Street, or even even M16, our much criticized Spy Agency, there would be major repercussions.

"The anti-terrorist branch of the Yard would be called in; overtime would be approved without the traditional hair-pulling and signatures in triplicate. Reporters would demand to know how security could be breached; news anchormen would lead off their telecasts with speculations that a splinter group from the IRA was 'at it' again."

"True," I agreed. "But Scotland Yard *is* involved."

"We must assume, therefore, that whoever is involved in these little trials has contacted them ahead of time. Phoned in a warning that something out of the ordinary was going to happen at such-and-so a place, at such-and-so a time. Very much like Burgess Meredith did on *The Wild Wild West,* when he caused earthquakes."

"That's right!" I fondly remembered. "'The Night of the Human Trigger' was one of my favorite episodes. Not only did it co-star my favorite actress, Kathie Browne, it contained one of the great classic ad-libs of all time, where Ross Martin made the quip equating "faults" in tennis to those associated with underground tremors.

It warmed my heart to know Gypsy and I were on the same wavelength.

"Among the questions we need to address are: why are these people perpetrating such a crime, what are their motives, where and when will they strike, and how much they're asking not to do it again."

Adding up the W's, I took a finger off the steering wheel. "You forgot one. And who taught you those journalistic ABC's?"

"That is the last," she pointed out. *"Who.* You supplied it for me."

Rolling my eyes, I went back to maneuvering my motor through the narrow, twisting side streets I had chosen as a shortcut.

An hour ago.

"Why is it I never get a straight answer to a question?"

As though taking up the slack in our conversation, the alley I had maneuvered myself into abruptly terminated in the proverbial dead end. Using language reserved for professional athletes, I threw the gear into reverse. The mechanism ground, hissed, sputtered and died.

I directed very ill thoughts toward the Czech Republic.

"That's it!" I groused. "I have every intention of leaving this rotten excuse for a car right here, a blight on the National Clean-up Effort."

"Your automobile does have one advantage over American-made cars," Gypsy helpfully supplied. "It will biodegrade in a landfill overnight."

I glowed like Times Beach at the thought.

"Here. Slide over into the driver's seat while I get out and push."

She obliged and I squeezed my way through the door. The peculiar thing about driving in G.B. is that most of the alleys through which one drives – the little back street passages through town that only a cabby with "the Knowledge" knows – are only wide enough to fit a car from the Czech Republic. Just try and get one of those fat, petrol-guzzling Rolls Royces through one, I dare you.

Now, for those of you who don't know, cars from the smaller, less industrialized parts of Europe resemble sardine cans turned on their sides. They steer with a wooden rudder, like one of those go-carts kids make from baby buggy wheels and 4X4's. You break the vehicles by putting your right foot out and dragging it along the road (remember how Fred Flintstone did it?), and the springs in the seat cushions remind you of lumpy beds found, the world over, in college dorms.

In other words, they're small, inefficient and uncomfortable.

Now, why, you ask, would anyone drive one?

Come on. You know the answer to that as well as I do.

They're cheap.

Yugo lovers of the world unite!

On the plus side, they're narrow and they fit through alleys with walls so close together you can smell the spray paint drying.

Now, most of these dwellings, with the walls nearly touching the sides of the adjacent buildings, were built by the Celts or the Romans or by aliens, way back when in the Before Time. None of those forerunners of Frank Lloyd Wright could have known that

2,000 years after they build the mews, motorized vehicles would be using the alleyways between them as cut-throughs.

Yet here we are, in the 20th Century, driving on roads built before the invention of the sandwich.

It boggles the mind.

And prompts one to query, why can we still drive over pavement set down all those years ago, while the highways made three months ago have potholes which could swallow an elephant?

The peculiar thing about my "motor" was that, when pushed backwards, the engine occasionally started of its own accord, with or without a key in the ignition. I suspect this unadvertised feature was built into the model as an aid to would-be car thieves on holiday from those middle European countries with long-sounding names and boarders which shift more than often than sand on a beach at high tide.

Don't think I have an ax to grind with these nationalities; I'm part Czech myself. At least, that's what I'm told. Czech or Yugoslavian and Scottish-Irish. People tell orphans lots of things which aren't true, but since I look like a combination of those peoples, I've sort of accepted it.

It's not a bad combination by any means. My gripe with my parents isn't my heredity, it's my name.

Or lack thereof.

But I digress.

"It's started!" Gypsy called, rousing me from my reverie. Huffing and puffing from the mental exertion, I pulled back in surprise, saw, or rather heard, she was right, and scooted back into the car, this time into the passenger's seat.

"Are you sure you can drive this thing?" I worriedly inquired. "It's not mine, you know."

"Oh? You are one of those car thieves from a middle European country on holiday to steal automobiles from hard-working Englishmen?" I started to protest, then gave up. "I am delighted," she continued, gunning the engine and shooting ass-backwards through the alley like Lee Petty (going forward) at a NASCAR race. "This is wonderful news!"

I had to ask.

"Why is that?"

"Then you are part Gypsy. Everyone who steals is considered an extended member of Gypsy Nation. Have you ever stolen, or eaten, an infant?"

I pouted.

"No."

"That is too bad. I shall give you the recipe."

It was my own fault. I was the one who kept accusing her of stealing babies.

"I'm sorry," I sighed.

"Oh, do not be sorry," she chatted, as easily as though we were not going seventy-fives miles an hour in reverse through an alley the width of two Popsicle sticks. "Gypsies and elves have the same bad rap."

"Bad rap?"

I hadn't heard that expression since hitting the wrong radio station. Or was it Watergate?

"Elves are always accused of stealing little human babies and replacing them with even smaller, ugly elf babies." She grunted in annoyance. "Have you ever seen an ugly elf?"

I had to admit I had not.

It was that ethnic consciousness of being part Irish.

"Ask yourself: why would an elf want a human baby? They are too big to fit in a hollow tree, they are loud enough to drown out Elf Family Network Cable TV programmes. And, there are no Elf Pampers large enough to accommodate one. Think what that means to the elf janitors."

"You have a point."

"Nor are Gypsies like Shakers. You know what a Shaker is?"

My first thought was "salt," but I had gone to college in New York and had done some early reporting around Albany (the capital, for all you ignoramuses who do not come from the Empire State). The Shakers were very big around that area. There's even a refurbished Shaker house adjoining Albany Airport.

Who said county planners didn't know what they were doing?

"Yes. I know about the Shakers. They didn't believe in reproducing themselves, so the only way they could keep the sect going was to 'recruit' orphans."

Even if I had never covered the dedication of Rockefeller's Pyramid, Albany, I would have known about the Shakers. Orphans know all about 'adoption agencies' through the ages.

I would be a Shaker today, if one of them had come and offered me a home.

"Gypsies are very romantic, sensual people. We do not need to steal babies to maintain our way of life."

There was no way I was going to argue with that.

The car shot out into a main thoroughfare (in reverse), crossed a median (fortunately low, for the car had a ground clearance about the height of a praying mantis), narrowly avoided an oncoming lorry (which looked, to my terrified eyes to be about a 200-wheeler), rolled onto the shoulder and finally came to a stop, it's engine purring like a jaguar (small "j").

"That was fun!" Gypsy declared, rubbing her hands together and looking around for the checkered flag.

"Gypsy, have you ever driven before?" I panted, trying to quell my erratic heartbeat.

"Yes!" she declared in that tone of voice I was getting to know so well. "Back home, I was considered a whiz behind the reins of a four-up!"

I deposited the contents of my lunch along the side of the road, we exchanged places and I "carried on."

That was a big expression back in the Days of Yore. No matter how serious your illness, or how traumatic a shock you sustained, you were expected to Carry On.

As though our caregivers were raising a generation of Marines.

It was all Eisenhower's *fault.*

Which had nothing whatsoever to do with either tennis or earthquakes.

We arrived back at her place in time for an early supper (a word interchangeable with "dinner" in the States, but not so in Europe), then Gypsy had some clients to see. I dearly wanted to watch, but she discouraged me. Then I knew she must be entertaining some real doosiers, wishing to communicate with a former butler on the proper procedure for ironing the master's trousers, or seeking to know whether the map they bought on the Florida Panhandle with a large "X" would really lead them to buried treasure.

I knew Gypsy knew I'd want her to tell them "Yes!" People like that deserve to be taken. To exactly the same place her first clients were going.

With a nod of the head to Margaret Mitchell, they don't make "butlers" like they used to.

Left to my own devices, I decided to go out for a nightcap. Not hard liquor: I left that sort of carousing for Mike Hammer. I was thinking more about a latte with a dusting of cinnamon over whipped cream.

I tried *La Boutique* again, and found it hopping. This raised my spirits a bit, but upon closer inspection, I noticed none of that earlier crowd appeared to be partaking their java-on-the rocks there. There was also a different milktender on duty. I had an idea what I wanted to do, but had to work up the nerve. It was not exactly approved investigative technique.

Ambling up to the bar, I waited until there was a lull in traffic, then leaned across the highly polished wood, which, to my untrained eye, looked as though it had been manufactured using an endangered species from a rain forest. I gave the man behind it a smile.

"Hello," I began.

"You looking for a job?" he suspiciously demanded. I was appalled and quickly smoothed down a strand of unruly hair, least he think I was too poor to afford a stylist.

"No. I have a job. A good job," I added, rapidly rewriting my preplanned dialogue. Like other preplanned ventures – funerals come to mind – this one died an early death. "That's what I wanted to talk about. Money."

Forget little hand-held communicators. Everyone knows moolah is the Universal Translator. It opens more doors than any machine which can help you say, "Take me to your leader" in two hundred, thirty-seven different alien languages, including Romulan and Klingon.

(Vulcan, as we all know, cannot be spoken by the Human tongue.)

His eyebrows arched, so I knew he was familiar with "Amok Time."

What about money?"

"This girl I met in here the other day. She asked me for a loan. I gave her what I had and she promised to come back here after I got paid."

Had I been wearing pinstripes, I would have said, "After I borrowed off the interest in my Trust Account," but I had a feeling that wouldn't wash, coming from a guy in a rumpled summer suit and a polka dot tie.

The points of interest in the man's eyes turned into cans of Raid. He indicated the highly stylistic chalk board behind him, where menu prices were listed.

"Honey," he purred, "None of the kids who come in here need money. If they did, they wouldn't borrow it from you."

Class consciousness at its worst.

"OK," I admitted. "I saw a good looking chick last time I was in here, and wanted to resume our conversation."

"Dads," he said with a well-worn sigh. "You're wasting your time. And mine."

I threw up my hands in resignation and tried my most affable, toothless geriatric grin.

"There's no fool like an old fool. You think a tattoo would help my chances? Put me onto a good artist, won't you?"

To his credit, he didn't laugh. I guess, in the tradition of bartenders everywhere, he had heard them all.

"Down the street, turn left, turn left again, turn right, walk past the dog groomer's place, then follow the signs. And good luck," he added, breaking with tradition by giving me a hearty guffaw.

And thus losing the fiver I had in my hand.

With a brave "Cheerio," I hastened away.

Left, left, right, past dog groomer, follow signs. It took me two tries and ate up nearly three quarters of an hour before I discovered my error. It was not in the "lefts," the "right" or "past the dog groomer," but in the "down." In my innocence, I had taken "down" to mean, in the direction street numbers decreased. Apparently in this topsy-turvy world, "down" meant exactly the opposite.

I guess it was some Marxist thing having to do with political rights and lefts.

I found the dog groomer, who, by the way, could have benefited from employing a dog cleaner-upper, but didn't find any "signs" to follow. But then, in my old-fashioned manner, I was looking for signs, as in advertisements.

Men: Express Your Virility With A Snake Tattooed around your Biceps!

Women: Reveal Your Femininity With A Rose Tattooed where your Father will never see it!

Blokes: Seven Hundred styles of beer cans available for immediate imprinting! All international brands available; Not responsible for Copyright Violation Laws.

In my ignorance, I wasn't sure if that would be a good or a bad sign.

Turning my back on traditional male reticence, I entered the Dog Groomer's habitat and asked for directions to the Tattooist. He looked at me as though I had just requested he do a perm on a beagle.

"What do I look like?" he demanded. "A directory?"

Common courtesy dictated I ignore his question.

Thanking him, I tucked my tail between my legs and left.

Being a reporter, however, I was undaunted by the fellow's refusal to help. Journalism 101 dictates that if the first twenty people you ask ignore you, the twenty-first will have the answer you seek.

I was not thinking well of school truisms when I spotted what I was looking for: a hitherto ignored series of dots and dashes carefully tapped into the side of a building. Knowing that Morse Code had been abandoned, I immediately (and correctly) assumed this must be a Sign.

After careful deciphering (it was written in that ornate Olde English scroll people like so much for letterheads because it makes them seem like a baron or a Name), I read the words aloud: Follow The Yellow Brick Road.

Auntie EM was with me.

There actually were bricks painted yellow. The pavement was one of those really old roadways inlaid with brick that you can still find on out-of-the-way side streets. Most were worn and more than a few were missing but I had no trouble following the yellow trail. It led me to a dilapidated, free-standing three-story building, dedicated to small shops. The tattooist, I was informed by more scrolled words, was on the second floor.

When I knocked on the door of the business on the second story, then popped my head in after receiving no answer, I found myself in a Black Arts and Mysticism Emporium. The smell emanating from it was horrific. Being used to incense from Gypsy's frequent use of that mind-altering drug, I knew the stench was not coming from a smoldering punk, much as I would have wished.

Rather, it was coming from those substances generally declared illegal, but commonly available, the world over.

"Tattoos?" I inquired without inhaling.

"Second storey," the man grunted.

"I'm *on* the second story," I protested. He gave me a "thumbs up," using an alternate finger. I departed rapidly and climbed the last set of rickety stairs that couldn't have passed a fire law inspection given by Mr. Magoo.

I had forgotten that in England, the first floor was located on the second story, making the second story of the dwelling on the third level.

It was getting easier and easier to see why the sun had set on the British Empire.

The tattoo parlor was a thing of beauty and a joy forever. Lining the walls were photographs of people, all of whom had (presumably) been tattooed by the artist-in-residence. Beginning on the left, the pixs depicted a nude man so completely black and purple from tattoos, I expected a baby alien to emerge from his stomach. Following him was a woman who, in polite company, would not have been able to show off one single tattoo.

There were snake men, walking encyclopedias of dog breeds, a person (gender un-guessable) sporting (it was alleged) 1,283 daisy chains, permanently engraved in various (fading) colors of white (technically not a color), orange, yellow and green (stems). Without thinking, I reached out to pluck a petal.

"She loves me, she loves me not."

"That's what they all do," a voice behind me announced with approval. Spinning on my heels, I was met by the artist himself, a man so wizened and horizontally challenged he could have passed for a Munchkin.

"Nice, ain't it?" he continued, utterly nonplused by my reaction.

"Looks very real," I agreed.

"Come for a tattoo?"

"Come to check out your catalogue."

"Help yourself. Lookin's free."

Walking further down the line, I encountered lionesses mating, bear cubs standing on their hind legs, toads, frogs, numerous styles of Union Jack, anatomically incorrect male reproductive organs, stenciled breasts on males, faux diamonds on foreheads, crosses, peace symbols, hot rods, lucky numbers and lots and lots of "Mom's" and hearts, inevitably pierced by arrows.

"Lookin' fer somethin' specific?" the artist inquired. "If you don't see what yer lookin' fer, I got books with pictures in 'em."

"Something small to begin with," I hedged. Then, with trepidation, "Does it hurt?"

"I got a topical anesthetic, helps some. After a while, the body gets used to the pain and you don't feel it no more."

"Expensive?"

"Depends on what you want. Now you..." he began, sizing me up, "are in love. You want to impress a girl. That right?"

"That's right," I agreed, smiling toothily at him to cover the headache I was developing. "You see, I'm a little old for her – at least she thinks so. I want to do something – wild – you know – out of the ordinary, to impress her. She has a tattoo," I added. "I thought if I got one, too, she'd take me more seriously. I really do speak their language," I added, trying to sound both sincere and square at the same time.

"Where'd she get her ar-teest work done?" he suspiciously inquired.

"I don't know. Here, I think."

"What's her name? I can look her up in my records." He tapped forefinger to head, indicating that's where he kept his records.

"I don't know. But she's beautiful. She shaved her head – I'm into phrenology, you know. I could tell by her bumps that she was an extraordinary human being. I wouldn't be surprised if her skull compared favorably with Napoleon's."

"The tattoo," he patiently reiterated.

"A snake, squirming around her temples."

He thoughtfully nodded.

"What kind of snake?"

"Are their different kinds?" I nervously asked.

It wasn't that I was afraid of snakes; I was scared I wouldn't be able to escape without him inscribing a mouse on my behind.

"Sure there are; lots o' different kinds. Makes a big difference. There's poisonous snakes, copperheads, rattlers, and little, innocent garden snakes. Want a tarantula?" he suddenly demanded.

"No." Then more softly, "She might think I'm being too aggressive. I'm a man of peace. Don't believe in killing. That's murder. Besides," I added more assertively, "If we drop the bomb, who'll be left to serve us?"

"Us?"

"Yeah; us. Those with the brains. We don't want to live underground. We're not for destroying; we're for preserving. We only have one Mother, you know."

I wasn't sure what the little man was thinking and it made me nervous. I figured I had better find out all I could and scram.

"Do you know her? Did you do that artwork for her?"

"Maybe."

I backed away, hesitated, then turned my back on him in a gesture of good faith. I could feel him watching me with a pointed stare.

"I think," he finally decided, "You ought to try a rose. A small red one. Up here, on the shoulder," he indicated. "I think she would like that."

I hopefully turned back.

"Then you know her? You remembered something?"

"Or maybe a butterfly – on the tip of your nose. I work it right, I can use two of your freckles for its eyes."

"No," I hesitantly refused. "I'm not sure. Let me look around some more."

He shrugged and this time, left me alone.

I gave it another five minutes, then turned back when I felt him reenter the parlor.

"I just can't make up my mind. And what if she doesn't like what I pick? Tattooing is so... permanent."

He did not look pleased. I had a feeling I had done about as much looking for free as I was going to get. My shoulders sagged.

"How 'bout a statement?" the man asked in a last-ditch effort. "Something significant, like 'I love you.' Or how about –"

"Flower Power?" I suggested.

"'My One and Only,' under your heart?"

"What about something across my brow? Like 'Eat at Joe's'?"

He pointed to a stool and I baby-stepped over to it. Perching my posterior over the small, unpadded seat, I reached for my wallet.

"Do you take Blue Cross?"

ACT 8

Gypsy was delighted.

"Let me see!" she pleaded, grabbing me by the shoulders and spinning me around to face her. "A tattoo! How lovely. I am certain Mr. McGraw will be most impressed at the lengths to which you have gone to assimilate yourself as a native."

When she did not find "Eat at Joe's" across my brow, she pouted.

"You decided on a griffin, perhaps? They are red, you know; with all your freckles, you would not have to worry about improper color coordination."

"When he set that tray of needles down beside me, I panicked and ran out of there like my ass was on fire."

"You did *not* get a tattoo?"

"No."

She pretended disappointment, then tussled my hair as though I were a small boy having fallen off his new bike.

"Mr. McGraw will be disappointed, of course. But he will grow in understanding."

"If he had seen some of the tattoos I saw, he'd turn into the Jolly Green Giant."

I saw her grin and felt better. I was afraid she really had wanted me to get a tattoo.

"Kimbo, anything you did would have been all right with me," she declared. I started again at her reading my mind, then slowly shook my head.

"That's a dangerous thing to say to anyone," I warned.

"I trust you."

"Are Gypsies always this trusting?"

"No."

The bluntness of her answer both reassured and saddened me.

"Have you no other friends?" I asked. "Relatives? Don't you belong to some Mind Readers Society, get together, think about the

Pythagorean Theorem or something to blow their minds? Join Mensa? There was an *Avengers* episode about something like that. Mrs. Peel became a member and had to cheat on Steed's entrance exam to get him accepted. Very funny."

"You are very smart," she pouted, not appreciating my deprecating humor.

"Not smart enough to get into Mensa, baby. Now, answer my question."

"Oh, I have relatives – and many Gypsy friends," she counted off on her fingers. "I do not belong to any Mind Readers Societies, nor do I share secrets with Hocus Pocus performers, crystal ball gazers, Tarot card readers, astrologers or government officials."

"Ever go to the movies?"

"As often as you," she happily declared, having discovered more common ground between us. "Although they refer to the motion pictures here as the 'cinema.' You do not wish to sound like an outsider."

"I'll always be an Outsider," I truthfully avowed. "I was born different. So were you."

She beamed with pleasure.

"We will have 'a bite' to eat and then go to bed."

How could a red-blooded American who grew up crisscrossing the Canadian border doing menial labor; who was educated in the alien nation of New York City, was banished from L.A. and did hard time in St. Louis, Missouri, disagree with that suggestion?

Gypsy made chicken paprika and I supplied both appetite and condoms.

In the morning, I drank two gallons – excuse me – two-point-something liters of coffee – with sugar and light cream to lighten the load on my stomach lining – and consumed six pieces of French toast (I asked for the "Continental"), smothered with butter and maple syrup (or something of its ilk), and sipped on a glass of grape juice.

Gypsy matched my coffee intake, while consuming an egg-in-a-hole, a staple called fried tomatoes (which looked like road kill), and orange juice.

We were, after all both bachelors, and single people eat what they want, when they want. It's a Great Downside to marriage that one must coordinate one's culinary tastes to suit one's spouse.

Speaking with my mouth full (rather more like a married man than a lover trying to impress), I pointed out the sole flaw in Gypsy's preparations.

"Gyp," I declared in a rather stern voice, "this is imported New York State maple syrup. I hate to complain, but Vermont makes the best maple syrup. It is, after all, the Maple Tree State. New York is only the Empire State."

"Vermont," she tartly replied, "is the Green Mountain State."

"Is it? I guess it is. But you can't eat green mountains," I pointed out in self-defense.

"Nor can you eat empires, but England did pretty well living off its Empire for hundreds of years," she pointed out.

A point well taken. Any casual observer could note she and I were on the best of terms, and thus unmarried. We not only took the time to have a pleasant breakfast conversation, our disagreements were verbalized with calm, respectful decorum.

"True. Now: here is something you may not know. Note this maple syrup. It is amber in color and graded 'A.' Sounds pretty good, doesn't it? But it's deceiving. The grading system starts with AAA and works its way down to B. Anyone who ever went to high school knows a 'B' is an above average mark. A-B-C-D-E.

"The great marketing directors know this. That's why they grade maple syrup with A's and B's – it all passes. And the consumer is so uneducated, he thinks he's getting a bargain, when he's really getting the dregs."

"You would wish me to buy Aunt Jemima in future?" she asked, a touch of drollness in her otherwise kindly voice.

I scowled into my grape juice glass, noting my complexion had turned purple.

"I do not. That is not maple syrup. It is *faux* maple syrup, made out of brown sugar and water, or some such. And besides, it's the wrong texture and color."

"We in England are not class conscious," she reminded me. "London is the new world capital, where the blending of races is well accepted."

"I'm not talking about people; I'm speaking of pancake toppings, for crepe's sake!"

"Fine. The next time you make your own griddle cakes, I will see to it you have the correct color maple syrup with which to drown them."

"I'm only attempting to educate you! Don't you want to learn? The lighter a maple syrup is, the higher it's quality. Like grapes. It comes from the first pressing."

She drew back in a display of astonishment.

"Now I have learned something. Maple trees are pressed to make syrup. I would like to see that done. Perhaps we can get a docudrama on BBC-3."

"We are not amused," I sourly quoted.

"That is taken from a conversation Queen Victoria had with an ambassador. Did you know that?"

"No!"

"I thought, dear Kimbo, you wished to have an enlightening conversation. You educated me and I have educated you. Does it not work both ways?"

I got up from the table and wiped a bit of dark amber maple syrup from my chin. In a flash, I knew what had happened.

We were arguing at the breakfast table.

That meant we were in love and should be married.

Another irrefutable grading system.

"Come on," I invited, trying to soften the shock of the revelation. "Let's go to school and discuss power outages and rescheduled exams with the principle."

It was a tried-and-true diversionary tactic. Whenever things became too hectic at home, bring up the subject of earning a living. That always threw a wet blanket on any trivial fight over hard versus soft mattresses, carpooling, bowling, the lack of respect in today's children, or food preparation.

Married people understood priorities.

Single people just change their phone numbers to foil the bill collectors.

Gypsy popped up like a piece of toast, all smiles.

"I shall be through with my morning ablution before you have finished shaving," she announced.

And I knew we were safe. No married person could ever brag of *that* accomplishment.

We arrived at the Lord Sleet-and-Mist VII Grammar School at nine o'clock. Trying to phone ahead for an appointment had proved futile. The only number listed in the book was answered by a recording, ordering us to explain, in clear, concise language, why our little Honorable was unable to show up for class. When we were unable to supply such information, the connection was terminated.

In the U.S., grammar schools were for children between the ages of four and five to ten or eleven. In the U.K., grammar schools were for the older kids. I guess that's because the Queen's English took a lot longer to learn than did the President's Language.

Parking our car in the teacher's lot (unmarked, but identified by numerous Czech Republic automobiles and bus benches), we walked up to the front entrance. Outside stood an imposing statue of the school's namesake, book in one hand, punishment rod in the other.

"It is a *staff*," Gypsy whispered. "As in, leading his flocks to knowledge. Knowledge being symbolized by the book."

I took a closer look, but wasn't convinced. Perhaps it was the gleam in his pinpoint bronze eyes. Or the fact one did not educate sheep, one prepared them for mutton stew. More likely than either, was the chalk-inscribed inscription at the base.

Lord S&M.

That I could relate to, having had a few such educators in my own time.

"Spare the rod and spoil the child" may have been popularized by Samuel Butler (I bet you thought it was Benjamin Franklin), but it had been around a lot longer than that. They still debate the merits of spanking in the States. Personally, I think it would be simpler to fry them all in the humane electric chair. Or put them to sleep in the gas chamber. Or hang 'em high.

The proponents, that is.

Gypsy poked me out of a favorite fantasy.

"Shall we go in?"

Bracing myself for the inevitable rush of nostalgic horror every sentient adult feels when entering a high school, I nodded and followed her inside. I felt like a soldier revisiting the scene of a bloody battle he had managed to survive years ago.

I didn't have any medals but I had garnered a diploma. And survived to go onto bigger and better things.

The System screwed up with me, I guess. Not that I'm against public education – I'm not. There just has to be a better way.

Which makes me sound like a political slogan.

Never mind. Onward and upward.

Several inquiries later, we found the office of Master Dickinson-Higby. After reading the name on the door plate, I snickered. It was an involuntary reaction and earned me a thumbs-up from a passing student.

It almost made me wish I had an Olde School Tie to wear.

After several more explanations, a wait in the antechamber (sounds like it ought to be a bathroom, doesn't it?) and a half hour's perusal of "Modern Education in the U.K.," which an obliging student had amended to, "Modern Education in the *Y.U.C.*K." we were admitted into Mr. D-H's office.

"How may I help you?" he asked, without standing to greet us. I guess we either looked as though we couldn't afford to send Junior to S&M High or were in search of a G.D.

"My name is Kimbo," I began. "This is Ms. G&^%#," I hurried, muttering over the name I was sure he would find offensive. "We're reporters for the Enlightenment in Education News Service. We're here to investigate a power blackout you had two terms ago."

"I do not see why," he articulated in that chipped accent which could have gotten him a job as host of *Masterpiece Theatre.*

"We are doing a story on the 'Curse of Modern Civilization,'" Gypsy explained. "How today's world is dependent upon conveniences such as electricity – light and heat, for example. When your school lost power, students had to be sent home without taking their term exams."

"I seem to remember something of the sort," he admitted, as though we were slinging aspersions on the System he stayed behind to protect in World War II.

"Could you give us some details?" I asked as a gloom settled over the room which had, I suspected, once been a 10th Century dungeon.

"There is little to recount. The power outage occurred just as students were arriving for their examinations. Inasmuch as there was no light or heat, they were sent home and the examinations cancelled."

"What date were they rescheduled for?" I inquired, without having any real reason for asking.

"For when were they rescheduled?" he rephrased, earning my eternal loathing. It was one thing to criticize another writer's grammar, quite another to have a plumped- up Ichabod Crane correct mine. He continued as though he had performed a deed worthy of his exalted position.

"In as much as we were at the end of term and the summer holidays were upon us, it was deemed inopportune to bring the students back merely for finals. Therefore, grades were assigned based on prior classroom work."

"Meaning those who might have failed were given a pass?" I asked with less than subtly.

The principal took immediate offense.

"I chose to look at it the other way around. Those who might have raised their grade from satisfactory to excellent were deprived the opportunity. What exactly are you implying? That this unavoidable mishap was deliberately perpetrated?"

I don't know what shocked me more – his optimistic take on missing the tests, or his use of five pound words. Making my living as a professional writer, I had learned never to use more than a seventy-five pence word – and never, ever to string two such lexiconic concoctions together.

"No, sir," I hastily corrected his correct interpretation. "Just trying to get my facts straight."

"You are not British," he observed.

Which was either an insult on my parentage or a compliment on my thoroughness.

"I'm from the United States," I tartly elucidated him. You can tell I was raised at the north-eastern section of the country, for everyone else inevitably replies, "I'm an American," ignorant of the fact Canadians, Mexicans and those from South and Central America were also "Americans."

"Currently on loan to the U.K.," I hastened to add before he read any international complicities into the story.

"I have told you all I know."

I pasted my best George Smiley face over my sharp reporter's features.

"Please bear with me," I sighed, slumping my shoulders by the weight of bureaucratic obligation. "My editor won't be satisfied with anything less than total absurdity. I'm sure you understand."

I reached into my pocket and fumbled for the inevitable missing pen while Gypsy picked up the ball.

"You had the incident investigated, of course," she began, assuming a dialect somewhere between Ringo Starr and Margaret

Thatcher. "What did your engineers determine to be the cause of the power outage?"

He hesitated, then tried on a bureaucratic smile of his own.

"They did not discover a cause. Everything seemed to be in proper working order. The school was the only locale affected. The local power company authorities reported nothing amiss on their end."

"When did the power return?"

"By ten o'clock that night."

"After which normal operations resumed?"

"That is correct. Which was a pity, because the students were scheduled to put on a play that evening. Without power, of course, it had to be postponed. Permanently, I regret to say."

"Why is that?" I asked, looking up from my self-defeating task of trying to locate a writing instrument. "Do you remember the title, perchance?"

"I do not. I fail to see the relevance."

"My editor was a dropout from the National Youth. He'll ask," I cajoled. "Those who can't act, go into vocations allowing them to criticize others."

"The play would have received very good reviews!" Mr. D-H retorted. "I watched part of the dress rehearsal. Quite stunning, in fact, although the final act-through was postponed. I seem to recall there was some... consternation about the ending. It was in the process of being re-written."

I reacted with genuine surprise.

"At such a late date?"

"Genius," he stated, staring at me as one not included in his assessment, "is never satisfied."

To prevent me from reacting, Gypsy jumped on the statement.

"Ah. Then you do remember that much, sir. You see? A little prodding of the old memory-box often produces the most pertinent data."

Had he not been born with a Stiff Upper Lip, I do believe Mr. Dickinson-Higby would have rolled his eyes.

"I will see what else I can provide you with."

The Man Behind the Desk rang a tiny silver bell. At first I thought he was dismissing us, but as Gypsy made no move to go, I remained planted. It was good to be in the company of an expert. Like being in church. When you can't remember when to stand, sit and kneel, watch the guy ahead of you. He'll be staring at the people in the front pews, and they always know the drill. That's because they're the ones who tithe 10%.

If you're not a church-goer, think about baseball. If you don't know the game (shame on you), but you don't want to mess up in front of your boss who dragged you along because he didn't want to drink alone, stare down at the Box Seat section behind home plate. Forget about the men. They're only employees of the Fortune 500 Company that owns season tickets. They just show up for the free food and the unlimited beer. Women, on the other hand, always follow the action. That's because they're the player's wives.

And one of them is bound to be the manager's wife.

Unless you're in Kansas City in the late '70s. Then, she'd be in the nosebleed section, staring down at *you*. Not to see how you're reacting, but to try and gauge the play on the field from where you decide whether to cheer or hang your head.

Gypsy poked me out of my sport's reverie and my head jerked up just in time to see a secretary or a clerk or whatever they call pretty young things with shapely legs, bleached blonde hair and a scent vaguely between gardenias and animal pawpits emerge from an antechamber. She had eyes only for her boss, which gave me an idea how much he made as a grammar school superintendent.

Or how little she made as an attractive go-fer.

"That file," Mr. D-H announced, pointing with a stiff upper finger toward a prison-black filing cabinet. "Second drawer from the bottom. Pull it out and bring me the manila folder marked 'Plays.'"

For a minute, my mind entirely misunderstood to what he referred. And then I realized it didn't matter, as she stooped to conquer, revealing an extremely curvaceous rear end. After wiggling it in unconscious deliberation for a full thirty seconds, she successfully retrieved the desired object.

Bringing it back to her Guardian Angel (that is the Radical Right's term for a Sugar Daddy, isn't it?), she smiled at him and faded away.

Flipping through the heavy stock pages, he finally came up with what Gypsy and I were seeking. What *he* was seeking, of course, had just left the room. Leaving a trail of animal magnetism behind her which would, under the proper circumstances, make electromagnetism seem impotent.

"Here," he announced, "is the ad-vert-is-ment."

Maybe willing young women in tight skirts were his thing, but what he handed me sure rang my bell.

Bold, graphic blandishments in bright, 82-point italics proclaimed the title of the production which the graduating class was going to perform.

Auntie EM.

As the true professional I was, I fell dumb.

As the talented amateur she was, Gypsy was up for the occasion.

"What an interesting selection, but a bit – youth oriented? For your audience?" she suggested.

"It was an updated version of *The Wizard of Oz,*" he informed her. "A modern rendition, as I recall. Although the costumes really were quite expensive."

"But, the play did not go on?"

"Unfortunately, no. It would have played to a full house because all the tickets were sold, but without the lights it was quite impossible."

"Tragic and quite unexpected," Gypsy commiserated. "Was it rescheduled for a later date?"

The headmaster (do they still use that word?) shook his head.

"Impossible."

"Why was that?"

"We were at end of term."

"But, with the tickets sold and the costumes 'quite expensive,' as you say, I would have imagined there would have been some attempt to reschedule? The following evening, perhaps? Otherwise, the school would have lost its substantial investment."

"I consider your implication impertinent," he retorted, reminding me of my days in another principal's office, many years ago.

I smiled the same sort of smile I had tried way-back-when. The kind which melted the freckles right off my face.

Every kid has that kind of facial expression in his repertoire. What you're not born with, you develop it as you grow wise in the ways of grown-up people. Some kids are just better actors than others. They're called "talented," or "gifted," and great things are predicted for them. They're the ones who grow up to be professional embezzlers or learn how to marry for money.

The other kids – the rest of us – may get by with a few misdemeanors, but never reach the Big Time. We end up working in hospitals, or writing for itty-bitty news services.

"I have given you as much information as I deem appropriate to your original line of inquiry."

The freckles reappeared on my face as red splotches, just as they had when I was nine years old.

"One more question, if you will allow," Gypsy politely intervened. "The poster says the play was only to have one performance. Why was that? One would imagine a work of such magnitude would run a week or more."

She tried a smile which would have made Henry VIII turn Prince Edward over to the Bishop of Rome for his formal education.

"There was some issue with scheduling," Mr. Hyphenate responded with a frown, interlacing his long fingers and making a church steeple with his two pointers. His thumbs were crossed, however, indicating the church doors were still closed. "It is customary, as you suggest, to have the senior class write and perform a play that is performed the last week of term. Those students working toward their certificates in drama are judged by its worth. However, although I do not recall precisely, the theatre was otherwise occupied. Or, perhaps, there was maintenance being performed. Some time has elapsed since then," he stated without making it an apology. "One performance was agreed upon as being sufficient, although I imagine the students were appropriately disappointed, having put so much time and effort into the production."

Gypsy made a note of this stirring information, then dropped her pen on the floor. It rolled under the desk with a little help from her foot. I started to reach for it out of habit, but a quick restraining hand stopped me.

To my surprise, Mr. Bar-Sinister bent down to retrieve it. It took him a very long time to find what he was looking at.

Looking for.

"Here you are," he replied, straightening up and holding out the pen. It was purpously distanced from her, so that Gypsy had to reach the upper half of her body over his desk. As she retrieved it, my fists clenched, while that dirty bastard's church doors opened.

"Is there anything else with which I may assist you?"

He directed the question to Gypsy.

"These student-actors – the ones whose names are here on the poster – they were seniors? That have all graduated?"

He hooked his nose over the edge of the desk to have a better gander at the flyer which had mysteriously found its way to her lap.

"Yes. All very talented, very gifted students."

"They have gone on to University?"

He appeared pained for a moment. I supposed he had an attack of gas.

"Like many of our bright young people, that particular group has decided to take a year off before pursuing more advanced studies. To 'find themselves,' I believe is the expression."

"When I was their age, I 'found myself' on a chain gang, laying railroad track through the Canadian tundra," I muttered.

He finally looked over at me, his thumbs doing a back-and-forth movement as though to shoo away the unwelcome and the unworthy from the sermon on morality he was about to deliver.

"That, sir, is obvious."

Which came out sounding like the insult it was.

"Why is that?"

"You sit like a pugilist and have the shoulders of a lumberjack."

Now, ordinarily, I would have taken that as a compliment. Grading line and hauling railroad ties single-handedly was a talent upon which I prided myself. While it would never have gotten me into the House of Lords, all those blue-bloods with dwindling fortunes were living on their American (U.S.) wives' fathers' wealth, while I could have gone back to the Canadian Western and gotten a job as a foreman.

"Mr. Kimbo is the most recent recipient of the **D**uke **o**f Edinburgh Excellence in Journalism **A**ward," Gypsy supplied for me. "His work appears, under byline, in such publications as the London and New York *Times.* He is highly sought after by newspapers around the EU and the United States."

Gypsy didn't have to say that; I seriously doubted any accomplishment of mine would have impressed this Snot With a Tie. But for the first time in my life, I felt like Somebody with a Name.

Maybe I *had* made up Andy Kimbo; maybe I didn't know who my parents were or where I came from. Maybe I had worked like a dog, put myself through night school, shuffled from one newsroom to another. But with one simple statement, she had elevated me above all the titles, pedigrees and diamond stick pins in the world.

For the first time in my life I realized what it was like to love and be loved.

I wouldn't have traded that for all the Kingdoms on Earth.

I stood up on wobbly legs and gave her my hand. She took it, knotting her fingers in mine.

"Thank you for the information. I'll be sure to spell your name right," I commented.

He looked appalled.

"You do not plan on using my name – in print?" he gasped. "In a newspaper?"

"On second thought, I wouldn't think of it. The newspaper is too common a place for your name to be found. Most of our columns are reserved for talented and gifted souls. Like the Queen's corgis."

We departed before he could ask for his precious flyer back.

Once outside, Gypsy bumped me with her shoulder. I responded in the way a real, red-blooded man would. I kissed her.

Full on the lips.

When we finally broke our embrace, she winked.

"I think," she said, "Mr. Dickinson-Higby – your DH – just struck out."

And then it occurred to me.

DH.

Designated hitter.

Struck out.

Good pitching always defeats good hitting.

The White Rat – another fellow with a made-up name – was on my side. He understood pitchers, finesse, working the count, out-psyching the opponent. He was the kind of winner who would never look down on guys who worked with their hands long before getting paid to use their brains.

No surprise. He was one, too.

Not a bad team to be on.

ACT 9

Listed on the bottom of the poster for the production *Auntie EM* were the names of six students: Eleanor Andress, as Dorothy; James Polle, as the Wizard; Timothy Button-Rhoades as the Tin Man; Paul Wiedenmyer as the Scarecrow; Noel Delaney as the Cowardly Lion and Mary Keswick as Toto.

"Such common-sounding names," I observed, shaking my head. "Only one hyphenate between them. They could be anybody's kids, from a family in Akron Ohio, to one in Hyde Park." I shrugged. "What's in a name?"

"They may be just what they sound like," Gypsy warned. She was good about that, playing off me, devil's advocate one moment, rah-rahing the next. We made a great team.

"They may be. Interesting order to this cast, though: Dorothy comes first, naturally, but she's followed by the Wizard and then the Tin Man. While I don't remember exactly, I thought the Scarecrow usually took third billing."

"And Auntie Em is not mentioned at all," Gypsy observed, a fact I had overlooked.

"You're right. Peculiar. I'd sure like to get my hands on a copy of that play. I'll tell you what – I'll hit some of the local book shops, see if I can locate the playbook. It's not uncommon for students to publish their work as part of a graduation project. You make some phone calls to the theatres which were hit by the power outage. Ask which plays were running at the time. And who was starring in them. We may find a connection."

She wisely bobbed her head.

"You do the leg work, I do the finger work. Is that because you have nicer calves than I?"

I grinned.

"No way. You do a better British accent; I sound like a tourist. You know what people think about tourists."

"Leave your green at the state border and go home," she agreed. I looked up quickly.

"Have you ever gone through the state inspection from Arizona to Southern California?"

"No. But you have. I read it –"

"Never mind where you read it. And stop reading my mind!"

"Why? It saves time. Also, it always makes it easier. You are agreeing with yourself."

"True enough. But I already know I agree with myself. I want your opinions. Besides, there are things in here," I added, tapping my noggin, "which I do not want you to know."

"What things?"

So, of course, I started thinking of exactly what I desired to keep hidden. I could feel her poking around in there, the way a cat shadows through a dark corridor, looking for a tender morsel.

"Stop that!"

"I want to know all about you," she softly protested.

"And I want the right to present myself to you the way I see myself. Not the way others do."

"I do not pick up the thoughts of others, only yours."

I wasn't sure that was true, but didn't want to argue the point.

"But I react to what I think others are thinking. And you can read those perceptions."

"You need have no fear."

It was not what she said, but how she said it, that convinced me she had already read too much. Feeling exposed, like a book someone picked up and read the first and last chapters of, without bothering to wade through the intervening story, I back-stepped away.

"No one is exactly who or what they pretend to be. We all wear masks when we face the public. Most of us even put on a disguise when we stare into the mirror. We see what we need to see, not necessarily what's there. We assume one persona for ourselves and another for the world. That is..." I floundered. "Anyone's right," I lamely concluded.

"Do you really believe that?"

"Yes. I do. We're all actors in one way or another. Usually many ways. The doctor who doesn't have a clue what's wrong with a patient puts on a reassuring face; the supervisor whose mind is on Pimlico sits in a director's meeting discoursing on quality assurance. The teacher who thinks little Johnny is a dolt, praises him to the hilt because his parents are big in the P.T.A.

"What would the world be if the doctor came into the examination room shaking his head, the supervisor announced that he didn't give a fig about anything but increasing his own bottom line, and the teacher blew little Johnny off?"

"More honest?"

She exasperated me.

"In your scenario, Gyp, the patient would become depressed because no one knew how to help; the supervisor would get fired, and little Johnny's parents would end up sending him to a private school where people knew how to handle rich brats."

"Or, the patient might find a physician who could discover a cure; the supervisor might be replaced by someone who cared and Little Johnny might learn how to stand on his own two feet, without hiding behind his parent's influence."

I stared at her in dumb wonder.

"What about you?" I accused. "You pander to a clientele who want to hear voices from the dead and buried, answer questions about phony treasure maps and play on people's superstitions by stinking up your place with incense and black cats."

"My cat does not stink."

"You know what I mean. For a few bucks, you play the part of a fortune teller. The same way I play the role of a reporter. We all have to earn a living, baby."

"I think," she said, "that in your deception, you have deceived yourself."

"Save that for the *Oxford Dictionary of Quotations*," I groused, feeling naked and confused.

"Andy, I *am* a Gypsy. I *can* read fortunes."

"And if someone came to you with a terminal disease asking how long they were going to live, would you tell them?"

"That is interesting. You began your sentence with a singular – someone – then modified it to the plural, so as not to be forced to use a gender. To be grammatically correct, you should have said, 'If someone came to you with a terminal disease asking how long he/she were going to live, would you tell him/her'? Why did you do that?"

"Don't answer a question with a question!"

"I do not always see events as precisely as you suggest."

I saw that as an evasion.

"But if you did?"

"Yes. I would tell him – or her."

"No one can handle the exact date and time of their own death. They – that person," I amended, "might go crazy."

"If that person came to me seeking such information, that would mean to me, he or she needed to know. I would tell him. Or her. I believe in honesty. And you do not?"

I faltered.

"Yes," I picked through my word choices. "But in moderation."

"You? A reporter, who has spent his entire career seeking truth where others would hide it? You, who lectures Mr. McGraw on the need to inform the public? You, who storm into police briefings, demanding to have that which they would hold back? You, who have lived your life not knowing who your parents are because the Law, in its Infinite Wisdom, has withheld such knowledge from you?"

She hit me where it hurt, so I struck back where it hurt – at myself.

"I'm the guy who looks in a mirror and sees a freckle-faced man with unruly red hair and a passable looks. I tell myself I'm good looking so I can face the world. Me, the guy whose 'real' name is some State-sanctioned XYZ. Me, who dreams of writing the great American novel while I work for some third-rate wire service.

"If I had to acknowledge who and what I really am, I wouldn't be able to go through the front door, much less to work."

Her shoulders sagged, so I knew I had her.

"I think you are the most handsome man who ever lived. I love your freckles and your red hair. They suit you. I cannot imagine you any other way. As for your name, choosing your own is not a lie; it is your right to call yourself anything you are comfortable with. And you are a brilliant writer. Whether you write that novel, and whether or not anyone ever reads it, does not alter the fact you are gifted."

"Gypsy," I cried, holding my hands to my face, "when I was a kid, the other kids – orphans like me and no better looking, I might add – taunted me, made fun of me. I was different. Not just in looks. I stood out in a crowd because of what's inside me, what drove me, even then. But it hurt. It still does. So I have to pretend it doesn't. I learned to use my looks as a tool. 'Here's that tough mug who runs on high all the time. He's a jerk and doesn't even know it.' But they leave me alone, for the most part, because I pretend what they think doesn't matter.

"I picked my own name – a stupid name, as it turns out – as another defense. As part of my self-image, because I hated those who named me. I wanted something to call my own; something with dignity."

I bitterly laughed.

"Because I care so deeply about so many things, I have to play the clown. I have to downplay what I'm really thinking, pretend to go along, or they'll send me to the nut house. No one cares, anymore. They just want to get by. I don't play that game very well," I added, "but I try. So people can say, 'There's Andy Kimbo. He's just like us.' It helps me get through the day.

"And as far as my writing goes, if no one ever reads it, then it's a totally wasted effort. A delusion on my part. 'If a tree falls in the forest and no one hears it, does it make a noise?' I answer, 'what difference does it make?' When they cremate my remains, what will I care if someone says, 'He was a great writer.' They didn't say it to me while I was alive; I never changed the world. So I failed."

"I think you are confusing the meaning of life with worldly success."

"Life only has meaning – as you put it – if you believe in an afterlife. Which I don't."

"That is not true. As a reporter, you have exposed much evil, for the benefit of Mankind. As a human being, you have touched the lives – the here and now, if you prefer – of many people. You are not a clown, pretending to care. You *do* care. Deeply. Your pretense is not falsity, Andy, it is merely a cover for your true emotions.

"You speak ill of Sweet McGraw, yet you love him. And he loves you. You have enriched one another's lives. You say you have scorn for those with whom you work, yet you listen to their problems, not from social politeness, but because they are a part of your world.

"You investigate corruption, not to earn a living but to make the world a better place. You write not for the masses, but for yourself, because there is that in you which is creative. I have read some of your fiction; you have touched me through it. So, when you die, your efforts will not have been wasted.

"You say you were taunted as a child because of your looks. But those children do not hold the standards of beauty in their hands. You knew that then; you know that now. We cannot please all the people all the time. That is not trite, but a truism. Beauty is in the eyes of the beholder. That, too, is true. To me, you are beautiful."

"But – what if I had never met you? Then I would still be ugly. My writing would still be useless."

"Love alters many things," she agreed. "But not everything. You must love yourself first, Andy. You may think you do not, but you do. It is that self-respect which enables you to continue living; to face those who would mock and taunt. We do not always get what we wish out of life, but it is in the trying where we – you and I –

excel. Disappointment makes bitterness, but it does not devalue our accomplishments."

My head hurt.

"I want what I want."

"That," she solemnly pronounced, "is the other component. Dreams. We are what we dream. To dream the Impossible Dream. Do you disqualify that, because Richard Kiley's Don Quixote was mad?" Or, she quickly inserted, "Do you not see him as mad? Do you see his as following the ultimate quest? I think you do. As do I. Dreaming is not only for the present, but for the future. The now and the hereafter. And it is not," she added as a further thrust, "only for ourselves. What we dream affects others. Do you not concede his Dulcinea was altered? Changed for the better?"

"Perhaps. But, he died, leaving her alone. How now, brown cow?"

"She had Sancho. And if she had not, her knight in shining armor remained alive in her heart where before her heart was empty." Her hands went... akimbo. "There are certain constants, dear Kimbo. Continue to work for the temporal, if you wish – it touches the ethereal which serves for all time, whether you acknowledge that concept or not."

"Now you're preaching to me," I complained, for lack of anything more substantial to say.

"We preach by how we live. It is a method of teaching, both others and ourselves."

"We were speaking of legs," I muttered, changing the subject. "I'm off to do my legwork."

"And I am off to do my finger work. Our paths will intersect."

"For truth?"

She happily nodded. I escaped only somewhat intact.

Which was getting to be a habit.

And as everyone knows, habits are bad for you. And hard to break.

If this kept up, I'd have to buy myself a "habit patch," so enough of it would seep into my bloodstream I wouldn't have to actually commit the deed.

"Habit patch sounds like hobbit patch," I could hear Gypsy saying. "And that is very cute. Like you!"

Cute. What an ugly word.

I hit Burke's, the local bookshop, in a black mood. It took me exactly twenty-two seconds, Greenwich Time, to lose myself.

There are few things in the world so compelling as a bookshop. I'm not talking about your local big box brick and mortar establishment. I'm referring to the musty old antiquarian bookstores of yore, where you can discover out-of-print tomes, authors who never even heard of the New York *Times* bestseller list, quartos printed on glossy paper and illustrations printed from wood-cut engravings.

Books from the past with hard covers, yellowed pages; books someone once pressed a flower in, waiting for you to find. Books harboring press clippings of obituaries, or love letters from lost passed-away writers.

Books which bring back the memories of other eras – ones in which you feel more comfortable. Written by authors no one else ever heard of, but without whom, you would feel empty and alone.

Great stories by famous writers, never published in their lifetimes; not-so-great stories by anonymous writers which fill your lonely hours far better than the best "novel-a-year" hackwork modern authors produce.

On the dusty shelves of obscure shops, you can locate *Martin Eden,* perhaps the greatest dissertation on the agonies of artistic creation ever penned. You can discover anthologies of American Renaissance, with a story entitled, "The Midnight Voyage of the Seagull," written by Mrs. Volney E. Howard, whose husband's name survived, while hers was lost.

Without ever having to worry about working your way past shelves and shelves of "adult fiction," you can pick up any book and read it for the beauty of language. Pushed to the back, behind novels the length of encyclopedias, you may find a well-loved, dog-eared edition of *Robin Hood,* written by Howard Pyle, the famous illustrator. You may remake the acquaintance of Jane Eyre and her brooding Rochester; squirm under the moral agony of a senseless murder with Raskolnikov, or traipse through the hot, steamy jungle with Lord Jim.

There is something about old books; pre-read books, used books, which stirs the soul. *Bleak House* is not nearly so depressing read from the crisp, mass-produced pages of a paperback; Moby Dick still swims, yet lacks the sting of the salt-sea air when from a page that has never been turned.

History seems dull and inexplicable studied from a school-issued text, but alive with the sounds of cannon and hums of swarming insects as "Stonewall" Jackson works his way through White Oak Swamp in a soldier's reminiscence, penned from the faulty but faithful memory that separated 1863 from 1888.

I had no logical reason for walking into Burke's Olde Book Shoppe. "Auntie EM," the play I was seeking, would not be found amongst its shelves, or displayed on a rack alongside the latest edition of *Cosmopolitan.* I went in for no better reason than to revive my soul.

To reinvent myself.

A little old man was behind the counter as I entered. He glanced up as the shop bell over the door tinkled, gave me a friendly nod, then went back to reading.

I bet he sold three books a week, and wondered how he managed to pay his lease. Were it in my power, I would have subsidized him. The world will be a much poorer place when little havens like this give way to the modern and the profane.

I was mentally thirty-something years old when I entered the shop and twelve by the time I reached the first floor-to ceiling shelf. With hands trembling from reverence, I reached out and took the first tome I saw. It didn't matter the title; all that seemed important was that it was a book.

An old, worn, much-used, loved book.

The book in my hands had a leather cover, eaten away at the binding and worn at the corners. All three sides of the exposed paper were – or once had been – gilded. Trying not to let the old man see the tears in my eyes, I gently rubbed the soft leather against my cheek, luxuriating in the feel of bygone days. When I opened it, my eye went, not to the title, but to the date of publication. There was none.

I suspected as much. Many old books never had a date of publication inscribed on or near their title page. It wasn't considered important then. People collected books for their content, rather than their future, "first edition" value.

This work, which probably weighed more than most children do at birth, was Victor Hugo's *Les Miserables.* I had read it as a teenager, sympathizing with Jean Valjean as he fought his way from injustice and prejudice to a small semblance of happiness, before losing it all in the end. Or so I remembered.

Forget the Sam Sheppard case. Javert was the prototype for Phillip Gerard, the police lieutenant obsessed with Richard Kimble's capture. *The Fugitive* was from television's real golden age, and I had followed the series, week by week, ignoring the inevitable love stories while concentrating on the real theme.

Fear.

It was something I understood.

Ironically, it was Gerard with whom I ultimately identified. No one could have played the frightened, innocent doctor better than David Janssen, but Barry Morse's characterization of an Indiana "cop" touched my soul. It was he who ran – from the ridicule of his peers, from his own sense of failure – because of his driving, all-important duty to bring to justice a man he honestly believed had committed murder.

I suppose, in a way, Lt. Gerard was – no – still is – my hero. I, too, have been considered "obsessive" by my fellow writers and certainly by all the editors for whom I have worked. I, too, have been driven to near insanity by a burning desire in my gut to find out and expose truth.

Truth, justice and the American Way.

I wasn't Superman. Neither was Gerard. David Janssen (bless him), insisted on an ending to the series, even though he was warned it would ruin any money the show might make in syndication. Kimble got a reprieve and a girlfriend. The One-Armed Man received his long-delayed justice. Gerard got to go back to work, burdened, this time, with a new sense of guilt for having hounded an innocent man.

Gerards of the world unite.

In point of fact, I did need a copy of *Les Miserables*. The one I already owned (Hugo, forgive me), was an abridged paperback I had pinched from a bench screwed into the floor beside a Traveler's Aid booth at some bus terminal along my desultory route to Nowhere, USA. Warped cover, stained red with ketchup and browned with coffee stains from having been used as a lunch table. The last time I read it, cover to cover, was when I was summoned to jury duty. I was living in Los Angeles at the time. That county summoned approximately 4,986 men, women and cardboard cutouts (the kind locals in the back seat so they can use the diamond lanes) for every two – or was it three? – weeks of onerous duty.

I never came close to sitting on a case, but I did gain a great deal of first-hand experience on how the American justice system worked, a terminal backache and a head full of Victor Hugo's stirring, long-winded prose and immortal characters.

I say I did not need a copy of *Les Miserables*. What I did need was a reminder of exactly who and what I was. Funny, to find yourself between the covers of an old book.

Clutching the weighty tome to my chest, I recalled Gypsy's words.

Disappointment makes bitterness, but it does not devalue our accomplishments.

My fires were re-stoked. I was ready to do battle with windmills and incidentally, any selfish wizards, yapping dogs, girls in ruby-red slippers, men without hearts or Auntie EM's I might encounter.

Now fully awake, I had tumbled back into my Dream.

I bought my book, exchanged a few words with the man behind the counter, watched as he wrapped the purchase in brown paper and string, then left the shop, a richer and wiser man.

ACT 10

I walked into Dillon's, "The Bookstore," shuddered at the hyper-modern, ultra-clean, sterile, impersonal, organized cluster of shelves (none of which went to the ceiling), hurried past the myriad calendars, glossy-paged magazines featuring pictures rather than words and "sale" items (nothing under 10 pounds – money!), to the Young Adults section.

They're not called "Children's Books," anymore because no one is born a child these days. As soon as toddlers are out of nappies, grown-ups expect them to behave as adults; that is to say, adults as in "do as I say, not as I do."

Being a child is considered degrading. In the beginning there was the one room schoolhouse where one size fit all, which evolved into kindergarten, grade- and high-school. Now, parents start sending their diminutive clones to pre-school. One reason, of course, is that Mom and Dad both work and there's no one at home to watch Junior. It's not legal to employ the telly as a babysitter (although much cheaper), so little Miss and Mister get packed off to Learning Centers.

Every study coming out of Think Tanks these days warn parents, guardians and educators (mutually exclusive) that the five-year-old who can't count to ten without using his fingers, identify the tertiary colors and recite at least one paragraph from Shakespeare (with or without comprehension) will be left behind. They might even FAIL. This is BAD. No one is allowed to fail any more. It's "Go for The Gold," not, "It's In How You Play The Game." All or nothing, baby. Just ask that wrestler who wept at the Olympics because he only won a silver medal.

That's the true, "Agony of Defeat," but it wasn't his shame, it was Ours. What kind of a world are we making, where second best is equated to abject ruin?

I found *The Wizard of Oz* in the same section as *Call of the Wild,* but I've gone into my opinion of that travesty elsewhere. It was a movie tie-in so had lots of pictures. Blank and white, of course. In this reality, Oz had monotone in common with Kansas. There was only one pix in color and that was Dorothy wearing the ruby slippers. They've faded over the years, you know. One of the original pairs is in the Smithsonian and it looks sort of greyish. So, if the publisher wanted to, he could have gotten away with printing this one in living b&w, too.

I bought the book, which, by the way, cost me four pounds and change, double what I paid for the hardback of *Les Miserables,* received my purchase in a non-biodegradable plastic bag and left, feeling soiled by the pure, pristine atmosphere of book trafficking.

It was not until I left that I remembered I was originally looking for a copy of the play, *Auntie EM.* Swearing softly to myself, I considered retracing my footsteps, then thought better of it. I didn't have the maturity to face *Modern Maturity* one more time. Besides, I foolishly realized, it couldn't be there. They hadn't finished the ending.

Brown-wrapped, and plastic-encased books in tow, I wandered up and down the streets of Modern London, the great European city constantly inventing itself. I felt strangely at home here, although at the moment, I was so totally lost I couldn't have found Big Ben without a guide book.

There is something about London – a sense of history, perhaps – that has never been lost amid the gleaming high rises, blinking neon and roar of airplanes flying overhead. I don't think you get this impression from any other major city in the world. Go to Manhattan and you'll never envision Indians selling the Island for a few strings of beads, or hear the frenzied protests stemming from the draft riots of 1864.

George Sand would never recognize her Paris of the 1850's, Fyodor Dostoevsky wouldn't even be able to identify his Russia by the names of the cities he once haunted, and not even someone as modern as Fritz Lang could walk through Germany and feel at home.

London, however, constantly reminded the wanderer of grandeurs past. The Tower still stands where so many of Henry VIII's wives were incarcerated, Buckingham Palace maintains the aura of mystery and power belonging to the Empire where the Sun Never Set, and Shakespeare himself, whomever he/she was/were, would still enjoy watching a play at Stratford-on-Avon.

I was a Wanderer, an Outsider, a homeless entity belonging to another century, a different time, where type was set by hand and newspapers, printing morning and evening editions, sold for a penny. Everything about me cried for a return to the era of horseback transportation and cobbled streets; where the greatest weapon of modern warfare was nitroglycerine, cooked in large vats from the powder of dynamite sticks, and submarines used battering rams to sink their enemies.

What had this damned new civilization we were all so proud of, come to? *Star Wars* missile defense systems ate up billions of dollars, were designed to combat a threat which it was too antiquated to destroy by the time it was deployed, while heart transplants saved the lives of the few and the lucky, while millions perished from AIDS and cancer. The wealthiest nation in the world had a poverty level equal to that of some African countries and within ten years, parents would "pick their sons and pick their daughters, too, from the bottom of a long glass tube."

Which reminded me of something *she* had said. The woman from the coffee haus.

If everyone were dead, who was going to do the menial labor?

This wasn't a generational difference, it was a mind-set run amok. It made my blood run cold.

Return to Oz.

The genetically modified sequel.

I was tired and discouraged. The legal, non-prescription, no-age-limit-high I had gotten from Burke's Olde Book Shoppe had worn down to a nub, leaving me feeling depressed. I needed something to perk me up.

Cafe signs were less than encouraging: Flavoured Tea with Ginseng sold here! Get a lift out of Ice-cold Alpine water! Freshly baked, No-fat Pastries inside!

Of course, I could have ducked into the Lamb Tavern, where blue-shirted men escaped both women and worries in the traditional, old-world, bend-the-elbow fashion, but I wasn't much for that type of release, either. Street drugs were easier to obtain than a taxi, had the benefit of being inexpensive and trendy and would have catapulted me into Happy Land. Better than penicillin, available without a doctor's prescription and holding within their needles and brightly colored capsules the promise of unlimited vision and creativity, I had decided long ago they weren't for me.

Vision came from the soul and couldn't be tapped by artificially expanding the mind. Creativity was a gift one utilized by inspiration and hard work.

OK. I know. I have a tendency to wax preachy. I'm all for everyone doing their own thing. Just as long as it doesn't interfere with mine.

Be a hermit in a cave and write obscure poetry in unknown languages. I'm all for finding yourself. Just don't make weapons – bloodless or otherwise – which destroy people physically or psychologically. And don't look at me as your next janitor.

I don't know why I stepped into the "Eminent Dough-Main Cafe." I guess because I thought the name was… cute. It was a play on words and I was a writer. I was also attracted by the large, bold-faced sign in the window: "This is a GM-Free Zone."

I had seen those signs all over London and applauded them. Contrary to what you might think about "no Chevys need apply," GM actually stood for "genetically modified food." A GM-Free zone meant that whatever they were serving in the cafe or restaurant or Mom and Pop Fish and Chips, was *a natural* – free from genetic tampering.

Like I said, I'm an old fashioned boy; I don't like messing around with genes, be they corn or human. Believe me, I'm not one of those "maybe there are some things human beings are not meant to know," characters, so popular in the 1950's science fiction movies. I think God (if there is one) gave Mankind a brain to use. If It didn't want Us messing around with DNA, It wouldn't have created any to begin with.

But that doesn't mean We know how to use this new-found knowledge. Look at fiber; ten years ago, it was the rage. People were stuffing bran muffins down their gullet in order to stave off colon cancer. Now a much wider and more thorough study indicates that fiber not only doesn't stave off anything, it may actually contribute to all kinds of nasty diseases, including colon cancer.

Which makes me glad I'm a jelly doughnut and coffee guy.

"Give me something real," I ordered, sliding my derriere onto a counter stool. (Stool, as in seat, rather than that normally associated with fiber....) The young woman behind the counter smiled at me, prompting a second look. She was one of those pierced people setting the fashion trend.

I bet she didn't have one single orifice without a hole in it somewhere.

"Everything we serve here is real," she announced, far from as innocent at it sounded. I coughed into my hand.

"How 'bout a BLT?"

"Black... Leather...?"

I interrupted her before she could put something really embarrassing to the letter "T."

"Bacon, lettuce and tomato. On white bread, lightly toasted. With mayonnaise and sweet pickle chips, if you have any."

"Something to drink?" she dubiously inquired.

"Coke – as in cola."

She raised an eyebrow, shrugged and went into the back to place my order. While she was gone, I took out my picture book and started flipping through the pages. I was so engrossed, I didn't notice her return.

"Are you into... *The Wizard of Oz?*" she asked, startling me out of my perusal. I looked up sharply, bit off my first reaction and nodded agreeably.

"I'm into peace, not war. Even if that peace has to be – enforced – with extraordinary methods," I stated matter-of-factly. She leaned over the counter, so close to me I could smell her tattoos.

"I wouldn't have guessed it, looking at you," she observed.

"Don't let the suit and tie fool you. I'm a veritable pincushion underneath."

"You are?"

There was new respect in her voice.

I nodded, smiling quixotically.

"Actually, I'm a writer. I'm doing a new play, sort of a 'socialist/pseudo-Main Line/Blow Your Mind drama,' based on the concept that all things are not as they seem."

"You sure talk odd."

"I'm an American."

The Universal Excuse.

"Oh."

Works every time.

"This play I'm writing – it deals with issues of today. Pertinent statements no one wants to hear."

"Sounds as though you're writing a play no one will want to attend," a young man commented, sidling in beside me.

"Herman Melville worked in menial jobs all his life; *Clarel* was self-published with money he borrowed from a relative," I remarked. "It probably sold six copies. Ever read it?"

"No," he informed me. "I'm an English major."

He wasn't joking. I swallowed ire in its tangible manifestation called 'bile,' and continued.

"Edgar Poe worked on and off as an editor, a publisher and as a writer. He made about half cent a word on his short stories; cheap, even for the times. He would have starved to death if he hadn't died from other, unknown causes."

"Who?"

I forgot I was speaking to an English major. I envisioned teaching in his future. As in, "those who can't do..."

Did I tell you that after journalism, English was my best subject?

"Edgar *Allan* Poe. 'The Raven.' 'The Tell Tale Heart.' 'Murders in the Rue Morgue.' I seldom use his middle name; it irritates me. Allan, actually, was the last name of the man who adopted him. Some say he was his father. His mother was a legitimate actress of the stage. Allen was her... patron? He disinherited Poe in his last will and testament, leaving the poor kid with nothing, when he expected to live like the Southern gentleman he was not, the rest of his life. Why should I honor Allan by association with one of the world's truly great authors?"

I had not meant to say all that, the words just tumbled out. My emotions spoke louder than words, but strangely, the youth leaned closer to me.

"You don't say."

"I do say."

"Now, maybe, it was Fate," my few acquaintance charged. "If the old stud had left Poe a fortune, the world would have been a much poorer place. There might never have been an Edgar *Allan* Poe."

I shrugged. Certainly, I had thought of that. It made me cringe, but I had a metaphysical reply for him.

"Perhaps. But, it's more likely he would have gone through his fortune in a year or two and after selling what remained of the family jewels, he would have been reduced to poverty. And that creative need which had been bottled up in him would have reasserted itself with the same bitter and tortured emotions which drove him to write his poetry and short stories."

The youth nodded with more sentience than I gave him credit for.

Or, perhaps, I was deceived.

"So. You're a writer? Ever get anything published?"

There was a loaded question, if ever I heard one.

"I've seen my name in print," I hedged.

"Yeah," another boy remarked, coming up behind me. "In the birth announcements."

I gave myself a minute to answer that one.

"Sorry, friend. When I was born, I was dropped on the doorstep of the local church. No one took the time to brag about my arrival."

That was more of the truth than I usually admitted.

"Got anything I can read? That you wrote, I mean? We've already read Edgar Poe."

OK. He scored points.

By contradicting his buddy, Mr. Who. And only incidentally by eliminating Poe's middle name.

"Like what?"

"Like a play."

I had, but they weren't for this kind of public consumption.

"Can I read it?"

"Sure. But I'm tweaking the ending. I want my work to be perfect before I present it to an audience."

"Any good at it? Editing, I mean. And finding the perfect ending?" the woman behind the counter asked, dropping her open-mouthed, dumb girl act.

"My best friend's an editor. He taught me all he knows. Believe me, if anybody can cut through the crap, it's him."

"So you write and edit, too?"

"Edit's my middle name."

"And what *is* your name?"

"Andy Edit Kimbo, at your service."

"But friends just call you Andy Kimbo, right? Like Edgar Poe?"

"Friends call me Kimbo."

"Andy Kimbo," the kid at my side repeated. "Akimbo. Right?"

"Right," I agreed.

"Made it up yourself?"

"I'm afraid so."

"What's your real name?"

"KB7608163."

That was actually Richard Kimble's prison number, but I figured they were too young to know any better. Besides, I never told anyone my "real" name. Not even myself.

"Got anything with the name 'Andy Kimbo' on it?"

He was challenging me to prove I wasn't lying to them. So far, I had been dancing around the truth, giving out enough of it to stay on the Right Side of God.

Reaching into my back pocket, I removed my wallet. I took out my International Driver's Licence (sic; remember *"Licence to Kill"* – my favorite non-Bond movie? It's all in the spelling.). The boy took my wallet from my clenched fingers, inspected it, nodded, then flipped through the contents, without my permission. I thought to grab it back, then stayed my hand. Peace may have been their "bag," but their idea of *pax* and my idea were universes apart. And they looked like they could back it up with some good wallops.

The boy at my side took out my most recent pay stub, read it, raised an eyebrow, then smiled.

"Andrew Kimbo," he pronounced.

Give him credit. He was an English major, after all. He could read.

"It's 'Andy,' actually, but people get out of joint when you use a nickname. It was easier to go along with 'Andrew' than try and explain."

"You are a writer, then," he observed.

"I said I've seen my name in print."

"With this kind of salary, you must have paid CANS to publish it."

I took his sentence as a joke and laughed it off.

"Know any writers who are well paid?" I countered.

His friend withdrew a bent and folded photograph from behind a credit card in my wallet. "Who's this bloke? Your father?"

"He's not my father!" I angrily protested. Sweet may be a lot of things, but I wouldn't wish that on him. "We're the same age," I replied, instead. "He's my friend."

"The editor who taught you all you know?" he taunted, correctly identifying the man in the photo.

Because *I* knew who Sweet was, it took me a second to realize my new friend had made a pretty astute guess. Too late for me to completely change what I was going to say.

"About editing," I lamely finished.

"What's his name?"

I didn't see any sense in lying, or I would have. I owed these people nothing.

"Sweet McGraw."

"What kind of name is that?"

"The same kind of name as Andy Kimbo."

"What's his real name?"

"He never told me."

"Ever wondered?"

"It isn't Rockefeller and it isn't Windsor. What else do I need to know?"

He handed me back my wallet.

"We could use a writer/editor."

"I could use a second job."

He picked up my book and studied it.

"What you reading this for?"

It was an open invitation to lie. Consequently, I told the truth.

"The Wizard of Oz is an incredible allegory. Most people buy it for their kids to read. It made a great vehicle for an already too old Judy Garland. But there's a lot more to it than that. Like *Gulliver's Travels.* Political satire and commentary at its best. So good, in fact, entire generations haven't figured it out."

"Like *Alice In Wonderland,"* the girl giggled.

I didn't see anything funny in it.

"Lewis Carroll was a child pornographer," I commented with less – I hope – bitterness than I felt.

"There's nothing wrong with looking at the human body," the boy at my side casually declared.

"There is, if adults get a sexual high staring at naked little girls."

"No exceptions?"

"None."

"Ever do an expose on pornos? In the newspaper? Get it published?"

"I did once," I gritted through clenched teeth. "But I never got it published."

"Why not?"

"Well, duh," I laughed, trying to ease up. "Why do you think?"

"Too many names named?"

"You guessed it. Does it surprise you?"

He shook his head.

"That's the way of it, man," he said, putting a friendly hand on my shoulder. "The higher you are, the more layers of protection you have. No one ever makes the P.M.'s pay."

I started at his abbreviation, my mind plugging in "E.M." for "P.M." As jigsaw puzzles go, it wasn't a fit, but it was close enough to be guilty by association.

"What would you say about bringing peace to the world?" his boyfriend asked, smiling benignly at me. If I hadn't been two steps ahead of them, I would have bitten, hook, line and sinker. It was, after all, my avocation.

Not a bad line. I decided to use it.

"This's my avocation."

"Want to work on a play we're producing?"

I pretended confusion, looking from one to the other. I avoided glancing at the girl behind the counter, however. If she wasn't Eleanor Andress, I'd eat my hat. Which, incidentally, looked more appetizing than the BLT she had placed before me.

Auntie EM was not only the title of a play, or a play on words for Electro Magnetic fields, it was, I deduced, in my best Dupan fashion, symbolic for the leader of this dastardly group. That would make Ms. Andress, who was to have portrayed Dorothy in the school play, the leader. Which also explained why the Wizard, who was, in reality, merely a powerless Professor, played second fiddle.

Everything in twos.

She was the one who wielded the power.

Which made it a safe bet she wasn't an English major.

As Whitey Herzog would say, never let the guy making the big bucks beat you. Someone's paying him a bucketful of money because they know he can get the job done. Pitch around that son of a gun and take your chances with the no-name, generic second baseman. It'll make you a genius, nine times out of ten.

Those were pretty good odds in anyone's game.

I nodded agreement.

"At what rate of payment?"

I sounded like Mr. Spock, from "The City on the Edge of Forever," but I figured they wouldn't know the quote, so I was safe.

And even if they did, I could always fall back on, "I Grok Spock."

They couldn't fail to "dig" that.

"I told you, Andrew – we're working for peace."

"... Justice and the U.K. way," I finished. "Yeah. I know all about that. But I don't believe there isn't some – pot at the end of the rainbow – you have your eyes on. I want in, and I'll edit your play – but I want 'A Piece of the Action.'"

I shuddered as my past caught up with me. I was on a roll. Never play *Star Trek* trivia with me.

The boys snickered.

"He says he's a pin cushion underneath," Eleanor Andress, d/b/a Auntie EM, remarked. "Heavily tattooed."

I grinned. Me and my big mouth.

"That true, Andrew? You one of us?"

"Why, I was just up at the Black Arts and Mysticism Emporium – aka 'A. EM.' 'A' from 'Arts,' and 'EM' from Emporium," I reasoned quickly. "Auntie EM."

They were impressed.

"You're in – for a piece of the action."

"Meet us here tomorrow night around midnight and we'll take you to our headquarters. See if you can really help us."

For peace-loving people, there was an implicit threat to his friendly invitation.

"Groovy."

They stared blankly at me.

I guess they weren't my kind of hippies, after all.

Su-prise! Su-prise! Su-prise!

Remember Jim Nabors saying that?

Did I mention Kathie Browne made an episode on *Gomer Pyle?*

ACT 11

"Gypsy!" I screamed, bursting through her door like a black cat with its tail on fire.

I had chosen an inopportune time to go postal.

(Is there ever an opportune time to go postal? Hardly for me to judge your actions.)

My palm-reading partner was in the middle of what I took to be a séance. The table was hovering above the floor a good foot, while the draped tablecloth shook and shimmered with scores of ghosts, poltergeists, disembodied spirits, long-lost dead relatives, inhuman FBI agents and nonexistent IRS auditors (see Book II in the "Kimbo, "Hold the Presses! Series), goblins, werewolves, mummies and vampires.

If you're keeping score.

The room was filled with ghastly noises, sounding more like tortured violins, off-key piano chords and reed instruments played without the reeds, while the air stunk to High Heaven (is there any other kind?) of what smelled to me like the East River at low tide, and was probably musk incense.

"I'm sorry!" I begged off, having the sinking feeling I had cost her a night's planning, an Oscar and two-hundred pounds – sterling. "I'm outta here."

Before I could escape, she called out to me.

"Kimbo."

But to my ears it sounded more like three-hundred pounds sterling.

"I'm sorry. I'm sorry. I'll make it up to you. Didn't mean to disturb the ghosts you were disturbing," I profusely apologized. "Tell your patrons I was in a hurry to speak to Joe McCarthy about a party I was planning, but it can wait until tomorrow. I haven't bought the masks, yet, anyway."

"Kimbo!"

Four-hundred pounds sterling.

I really *was* going to need a second job.

"Gotta fly. I mean – got to walk. Scram. Amscray. Travel. You know."

In my panic, I was running out of hip words.

"Andy. Stop."

I stopped. As in, "What is it you don't understand about the word 'STOP'?"

Everything. I'm a journalist, remember?

On second thought, better make that, "I'm an English major."

"There is no one here," Gypsy continued.

I looked around but she was invisible.

"My God!" I gasped in one of my more reverent moments. "I can't see you. The spirits have absconded with your body. All I can see is your voice!"

"If you can 'see' my voice, then you are in the wrong business," she laughed.

"Where are you, baby? Do you need help getting pulled out from the Underworld?"

"You are Eliot Ness?" she joked.

At least she hadn't lost her sense of humor.

"I mean – I mean, grab hold of my hand. If you can. I'll yank you back from wherever they've taken you."

"Good!"

She sounded relieved. I had arrived just in time!

Superman was with me!

I looked up. I looked to my right. I looked to my left. Nothing to grab. I looked down. And then I saw it. A hand, protruding from underneath the table. I raced to her faster than greased lightning (I never said I was health conscious), wrapped my fingers around her pitiful digits, struggling – womanfully – to escape the clutches of whomsoever had trapped her – and yanked.

Gypsy came flying out from underneath the table, hit me smack on the groin (fill in the blank for that generic euphemism) and sent me sprawling, to land, flat on my back. Fortuitously, she landed directly on top of me. Such a stunt would never had passed the 1950s sensors, but somewhere I just knew George Reeves approved.

"I've got you!" I cried, wrapping my arms around her, for fear the evil spirits would try and take her back. "Hold on tight!"

"A sensible idea," she agreed. "But if we are going to do *that,* I would rather get up and go into the bedroom. I fear for your back," she solicitously added.

"Not now!" I cried, unceremoniously crawling out from beneath her warm, voluptuous body. "Not until I'm sure we have banished Them back to where ever it was They came from!"

"Who – they?" she inquired with enough curiosity in her voice to make me blush.

"They – you know – the spirits who had you trapped underneath the table. The Whatever-You-Call-Thems. Don't look at me. I don't speak that lingo – you do!"

"You were doing a very good imitation of it a moment ago," she observed, righting herself into a sitting position.

"Come on. Let's get out of here until we're sure it's safe."

"Where shall we go? A motel?"

"I don't care! Anywhere!" And then I realized. And really flushed red. "You *were* being drawn away, into the spirit world, weren't you? I mean, I saw your disembodied hand waving at me –"

"Waving at you," she agreed.

I paused to catch my breath, which was not an easy feat, inasmuch as the ghosts had nearly ripped it out of my throat.

"Just exactly what were you doing underneath that table?"

"Putting a potholder under one of the legs. The table wiggles. I thought to balance it out."

Which put my sanity out of kilter.

Perhaps she could cure me, as well, with a pot holder. Although I doubted there were enough pot holders in the world to put me to rights.

"It is good to see you," she continued. "I have been waiting for your return. With baited breath."

Don't believe a grown man can melt into a puddle and sink below the floor boards? Catch me on the rerun.

"You might at least have taken Dandelo back with you from that invisible plane," I complained. "It's the least 'Al' Hedison would expect. Turn yourself into a half man, half fly, and no one cares. But leave a cat in a parallel universe and all sorts of people weep." Gypsy stared at me. Oddly. I guess she wasn't up on her science fiction movies. "Can I go out and come in again and start all over?" I croaked, wishing I could.

"Be my guest."

"I'd rather be – oh, never mind." I rolled my eyes and she helped me to my feet. "I found our little group," I informed her, instead.

"Yes," she nodded. "It is written all over your face."

"Is it? My God, I'll have to wash it off!"

"Andy, I was kidding. It is an idiomatic phrase, is it not? I have misspoken? You must correct me when –"

"No, no. You're correct. You mean, you divined it from my countenance."

"I read your –" I held my hands over my ears. "Eyes."

Amazing how holding one's hands over one's ears enhances the hearing.

"I need your help."

"That is what I am here for. All 'lock, stock and barrel of me'."

"Never mind. I need to be pierced. In a hurry."

She looked pained.

She should have been in my shorts. Err, shoes.

"Pierced?" Realization came in a hard jolt. Then she grinned. "An earring!" She clasped her hands together in joy. "You wish to become a Gypsy!"

"No! No, not an earring –"

"This is wonderful. I am so pleased. You will look wonderful with an earring. I presume you only wish to wear one, of course. I understand. That is traditional. I will get a needle and pierce your ear. Do you have a preference as to which one?"

I tried to envision Bela Lugosi from *The Wolf Man.* He was playing a fortune-teller-turned werewolf. It was a small role, but he stole every scene he was in. For the life of me, I couldn't remember which ear he wore his earring in. And then I remembered I was off track.

"Not an earring! Body piercing. Tattoos. I need to look like the in-crowd."

Fortunately, she did not break into song.

"You wish me to engrave you?"

"I'm not an invitation, for God's sake. Just a few – images. You know: snakes crawling up my biceps; a heart over my –"

"Sausage?" she suggested. I had seen that episode of *The Avengers,* too.

"We'll leave my 'sausage' alone. Let's stick to the basics: arms, chest. That sort of thing."

"You have very nice 'things,'" she protested.

"And I wish to keep them very nice. As well as functional." I had a sneaking suspicion tattoos had a lot in common with tight jeans – a walking advertisement, but they diminished a man's fertility. Not that I had any plans for such. It was the principle of the thing.

"Not real tattoos. Fake ones. Stencils."

"You want me to crayon you?" She sounded hesitant. "Are you numbered? All spaces marked with a '1' color red. All spaces with a '2' color yellow?"

"Not a paint by number. I'm not Mickey Mouse," I protested. Although, I felt like it. "I'm serious. I told those people – our Auntie EM gang – I was one of them. A rebel. To prove my point, I told them I was tattooed."

She nodded. Wisely.

"Good thinking. And you suppose they will check you out?"

I supposed so.

"They checked out my other story."

"Which was?" she dubiously questioned.

"That I was a reporter." She looked relieved. "And that I could edit their play; make a Pulitzer Prize winner out of it."

She frowned.

"It may become a best-seller, but after the fashion of *Mien Kemp.*"

"Obligatory reading, written by the master for his slaves. I know. But I doubt it will get that far. But you know," I added, inspecting my arms and judging best what tattoos would make me look like a sentient tough guy. "I wonder if it isn't more than coincidence. Hitler was an art student, ridiculed by his professors. He went on to become the most infamous dictator the world has ever known."

I rubbed my hands together as the image gelled.

"So, too, with these kids. They want to be great playwrights. Foiled in that, they'll take over the world by inciting a toaster insurrection."

I tried to smile, but Gypsy wasn't biting.

"Are you saying if Hitler had gone to a successful career as a painter, he would never have risen to power in Germany?"

"It's a thought."

"And if you help these Auntie EMers, you will prevent them from using their weapons against humanity?"

I shrugged. Put like that, my argument sounded a little weak.

"You," Gypsy declared with a sigh of resignation, "are a dreamer."

"A dreamer?"

"In the guise of a hard-boiled newspaper reporter."

I was shocked. One seldom cares to have one's self-image shattered.

"I am?"

She nodded. How was I ever going to be able to face myself in the bathroom mirror again?

"Not even a soft-boiled reporter?" I tried.

"You are cynical," she begrudgingly confessed. I brightened.

"That's better."

"Shall we go in and make love now?"

"After we save the world," I promised.

She laughed and I wondered if she didn't have a bit of cynicism in her, herself.

Getting myself "tattooed" was more painful that I had imagined.

"I think you ought to have a rose stenciled under your nipple," Gypsy decided, staring critically at my naked upper torso. "And you will have to shave off that chest hair. I do not see how I can work around it."

"All of it?"

She plucked at the coarse red hairs running crosswise from shoulder to shoulder, and down past my navel.

"No. I would not want to deprive you of your virility."

"Virility comes from a point lower than belly button," I pointed out. "I'm not Sampson."

"We will leave some to cover the images – to make it appear you have had them for some time, as if the hair has grown back after you were originally pierced. But," She softly demurred, "there is no way I can make drawings appear to be tattoos."

What's my option?" I whispered, less than bravely.

"I will use washable ink, inserted lightly under the skin. I suggest you do not take a shower while employed by your would-be world rulers."

"I wasn't planning on it."

"Lie down."

I did as ordered, and she began outlining her artwork. I squirmed.

"That tickles."

"What follows will not." That quieted me, right enough. "I will give you the traditional snakes and wolf's heads," she professionally decided.

"Just omit the 'I Love Mom,' please. And 'World's Greatest Lover." I didn't want to be called upon to prove either."

She ignored me.

"Perhaps a peace symbol here," she said, indicating the area below my heart. "But you need something unique... a statement. I have it! A poisoned pen! I will sketch an old-fashioned fountain pen, dripping with murderous ink."

I liked that. It fit my personality. I was already feeling better about myself. It's a wonder, what a little make-over can do for a soul.

Gypsy gathered together the tools she would use to transform me from a bland, clean-living boy into a walking picture gallery. Which reminded me – If I were ever out of work again...

"Add an 'Eat at Joe's', just to be sure," I advised Gyp.

"Where?" she asked. Which decided me to keep my mouth shut.

I discovered two things about being stenciled: I had a low tolerance for pinpricks and I was vain. Not very surprising but it made the procedure last well into the 11 P.M. hour.

"Are you satisfied yet?" Gypsy demanded, hands akim... on her hips.

I declared I was, although I might have consented to another snake crawling around my biceps. I liked the way the first two "hissed" at one another when I flexed my muscles.

"I never realized what a personal statement being tattooed is," I decided, glancing at my watch and realizing, with regret, there wasn't time for another copperhead.

"Then you will be relieved to know what I have done is permanent," she deadpanned.

The life drained out of me faster than a car doing seventy on the highway losing the screw from the oil pan.

"What?" I gasped, holding my throat, Zasu Pitts fashion.

Seeing the look on my face, she laughed.

"While it is rewarding to know you appreciate my artwork, I do not fancy living with a 'Child's Encyclopedia of Creepy-crawly Things," she declared.

"How long will they remain visible?"

"They will begin to fade after two weeks, depending on how often you shower. But, there will be faint outlines where the ink is heaviest for perhaps months to come."

The thought threw cold water on my enthusiasm. I had a sudden vision of my body, floating face down, in the Thames, the scorpions on my butt being the only survivors.

"I'm off, babe. Gotta fly."

"Do not try to sound too 'hip,' Andy. You do not fit the part of the World's Oldest Living Teenager. Be yourself, as much as you can. Remember," she continued, resting an arm on mine. "Bloodless warfare is the second coming: the modern-day reincarnation of the peace movement."

"I like that," I decided. "Can I quote you?"

"If you like. Wait a moment while I get my cape."

"What for?"

"I am going with you."

"With me? I don't even know where I'm going. Auntie EM & Co. is picking me up at midnight and taking me to their headquarters."

"Very mysterious," Gypsy agreed, nodding her head. "Midnight. The witching hour."

"You're not a witch," I pointed out. "You're a gypsy."

"Capital 'G,'" she corrected me, mentally translating my speech into the printed word.

"You're not a witch; you're a Gypsy for cripe's sake."

She grinned.

"I was not referring to myself, but I appreciate the thought. I meant Auntie Em and Company. They chose the witching hour to pick you up. That's part of their ritual – even for themselves. Part of the games-playing they're enacting. Don't you see?"

I had to admit I did not see. She motioned for me to sit, which I did. She followed suit, resting a hand on my knee for emphasis.

Or, from early stage training.

You can always tell an actor who's grown up on the Boards. He/she's the one who works through a fluff, smooths down another actor's hair when the ends stick up after removing a hat. instead of waiting for the director to yell "Cut!" He/she pantomimes pouring milk when the props people forget to fill the pitcher, sits down at a piano, taps away at the keys and hears the music, even though the instrument has been muted.

When you're performing in front of a live audience, there aren't any reshoots. You're almost as naked as the day you were born. Bawling like a baby when something doesn't go perfectly marks you for an amateur – or a film actor under forty.

Fifty.

Gypsy was a professional and so was I. I listened.

"I like the way you differentiated the true artist from the pretty faces," she admitted. I nodded before realizing she was still reading my mind. "It bears relevance to what I'm going to tell you."

"Go on," I motioned, leaning forward.

"Yes. You're right," she smiled. "All the world's a stage. The difference lies in which play the actors are performing. You and I are working on one level; our audience is what you might call the Real World. We're playing for those others who get up in the morning, go to work, come home in the afternoon and expect the world to maintain its equilibrium.

"We're fighting for the status quo – for the side of right, as it fits our values.

"Those young people – Eleanor Andress, Paul Wiedenmyer and their troupe of 'Ozites' – are assuming roles from an entirely different script. And for completely different reasons. Their denouement is personal attainment. They are trying to write an ending which benefits them, to the detriment of the World. You and I must prevent them from finishing their little drama."

The cadence of her voice as well as the psychological interpretations she was giving me filled my head with wonder and I soaked it up like a sponge.

"To live comfortably with what they are planning, they cease to become Eleanor and Paul, and actually function as Dorothy and the

Tin Man. As fictional characters, they do not have to reckon with consequences; the flying house will always fall on the bad witch; Dorothy will inevitably get home.

"This is both their strength and their weakness. As characters, they are infallible. Immortal. Everyone knows the lead players never die; and while they suffer setbacks, they ultimately triumph. They are not writing a film noir; they are all John Waynes, defeating cattle rustlers, misguided lawmen and unruly elements of nature."

She paused and stared into my orbs.

"Do you see?"

"They're nuts."

She gently negated my statement.

"What they are doing is not so very different than putting on a different persona to go to work; or, to romance a person they are trying to impress. They difference is, they have taken it to a higher level. The creation of their fantasies has taken them across the line between reality and unreality. They think by becoming characters, they have a right to act outside the law. Not just think it, Andy. They believe it."

"Thespian zealots."

"In a sense, that is exactly what they are. They have brainwashed themselves in the same manner as suicide bombers prepare for their final – and ultimate – role. Does a suicide bomber contemplate his own death? The physical pain and destruction of his own life? No. He thinks only of the final outcome, which he has been fooled into believing is the only true and proper course." She paused, and then added, "The ends justify the means. Do you believe that?"

"Of course not."

"Your little band of perverted Merry Men believe it. Perhaps their play began as an idealistic attempt to make a perfect world. A 'bloodless war' – isn't that what you said? A war where Right – their Right – the Right as pertains to them – prevails. Perhaps they were sitting around one evening discussing the horrors of land mines.

Such repulsion might have led them to imagine 'war' without death. 'War' being a means of social revolution.

"In order to stop the senseless bloodshed, they pooled their various talents and came up with Auntie EM – the power of an electromagnetic field which would strip human beings down to basics. Without airplanes, tanks, Star Wars defense systems eating up budgets better spend on medicine and education."

I nodded as I envisioned the scene. It was easier than I wanted to accept.

"It seemed reasonable to them, Andy. But at the same time, it took them away from their sense of what is right and just. It made them feel… entitled. Servitude without electrified wire fences, gas chambers and death camps is another form of hell. But, in their minds, they molded their outcome from care and concern to believing only they knew what was best for Mankind.

"They want to establish themselves as the new rulers, but without the democracy and the safeguards which governs the action of elected leaders. Separating themselves from the evil they perpetrate, they can no longer see their actions as destructive. By creating their own script, they are always right; they are the good guys in the white hats."

"I was never a big fan of the Duke's."

"Dorothy, the Tin Man, the Lion – lovable characters who ultimately got their fondest wishes. If, in so doing, they destroyed the Wizard's fantasy and killed witches, bats and well-defined evil characters, what was the harm? No one mourned the Wicked Witch of the East."

"Are you trying to tell me they don't know what they're doing?"

"I am suggesting it as a possibility."

"The other one being," I hesitated to point out, "they know precisely what they're doing and don't give a fig about what happens to the minions of the world."

Her eyes flashed a sense of hurt and I was sorry I had reverted to the Dark Side. Between the two of us, she had more faith in goodness than I did. Which forced me to seek a middle ground.

"Then it's our job to make them see the harm they've unleashed."

"That is where I would start."

It recalled to mind a line in a Bela Lugosi film called *The Black Cat.* The great Hungarian actor was playing a mad scientist, set on revenge. One of the characters he was intent on destroying cried out to him, "Try and be sane!"

It didn't work.

I wasn't so sure about Gypsy's plan, either.

And I certainly didn't envision myself as Samuel S. Hines.

But I was willing to give it a try.

ACT 12

We set out together, not exactly Don Quixote and Sancho Panza, but near enough, I guess, to put all windmills and future world dictators *en guard.*

We took my motor vehicle, which was tantamount to walking because even at this late hour, we still have to park half a mile away from the cafe. Gypsy didn't complain. I guess she was used to walking, and where she came from, even a Czech car was an upgrade from a pair of horses pulling a *Wagon Train*-styled Conestoga.

"This is where you leave me," I decided, stopping short of the Eminent Dough-Main Cafe. And you know –" I began, suddenly getting cold feet.

"What I know and what you know are two different things," she happily supplied for me. *"You* know this it is dangerous for me to try and follow you. I might be spotted; picked up and EM'd out of existence. I might be captured and raped by young men who think the world – and everything in it – is theirs to possess."

"That's it," I began, but she handled the situation just the way Christian Nyby directed the actors' dialogue on *The Thing.*

She talked over me.

"I know you may be discovered for what you are – a newspaper reporter trying to stop, rather than to join the Revolution. You may be EM'd out of existence. Or beaten, trussed up like an American Thanksgiving turkey, shoved into a black plastic garbage bag and ignominiously dropped by the side of the road, guaranteeing that no one will find you for at least two years."

She said all that without taking a breath. All the while, I was breathing hard.

"OK," I began but she came in on me again. (Did I mention that after 86 minutes, that technique tends to get on the nerves?)

"What makes your life more expendable than mine?"

"Because –"

"Do not go there," Gypsy warned in her best Helen Chandler voice. It gave me the creeps. It also made me think that even limited exposure to that Tyrannosaurus Rex of a police captain back in St. Louis, Missouri, had been a bad thing.

"All right," I hastily agreed. "We both have the unalienable right to throw our lives away. But be careful. Please?"

"I shall follow A. Kimbo's Rules to the letter."

I didn't ask what she meant by that. I didn't think I wanted to know.

Squaring my shoulders, I threw caution to the wind, waved her a hasty good bye and hurried down the sidewalk. London wasn't New York, where no one ever slept, but quite a few of these small shops – the kind which didn't cater to the tourist trade – were still open.

Loud music issued from the open door of the "Dough-Main" so I presumed it would be filled with people sipping GM-Free guava juice and munching veggie burgers. I took comfort in the thought. They couldn't all be members of Auntie EM. If I ran into trouble, there was a slim chance I could call on one or more of them for assistance.

Wrong. The place was as empty as a theatre running the end credits to a movie. I stepped inside, looked around in confusion, then identified the source of the music: a radio, perched atop the counter. It was loud outside, but inside, the vibrations rattled the walls. I don't know if it could have awaken the dead, but it sure would have covered the screams of the soon-to-be-dead.

There was little comfort in the thought.

"Hello?" I called over the din.

I didn't expect to be heard, but a head popped out from behind the counter. Being wrong twice in a matter of moments did not comfort me. You know the expression: three strikes and you're out. Well, it was 0-2 and if you don't know who was umpiring behind the plate, ask a Cardinals fan. One who remembers the 7th game of the 1985 World Series against the Kansas City Royals.

(Hint: it was the same man who had umpired first base during the 6th game of that same World Series. Or call 1-800-Ask-DaRat.)

Just kidding. About the phone number.

"Right on time," a smiling face declared. "Exactly as we expected."

"Why is that?" I asked, piqued, despite my resolution to be calm, cool and collected.

It was the kid I had pegged for the Wizard – the guy who took second billing in *Auntie Em,* after Dorothy.

"You 9-to-5 paper-pushers are all alike. You're the punch-the-clock generation. You run your lives by the rules."

"I never punched a clock in my life," I lied. "Knew a guy once who punched a fan, but that's another story altogether. You wouldn't know anything about it. It deals with right and wrong and personal frustrations."

"You think I don't know about frustrations – mate?" he lightly inquired.

I tried my most affable smile.

"You live in a generation of 'mobiles' and Viagra. What have you got to be frustrated about?"

"I'm clean, mate," he said, holding his arms out in brotherly fashion. "You're talking about what we're against."

I would have bet my paycheck that in five years he'd be the first in line for his prescription. But I didn't say so. It wasn't my intention to antagonize.

"So? I'm here and ready to rock n' roll. Where are the others?"

"Right behind you, mate," a deep voice replied. It was one I hadn't heard before. Spinning on my heels, I stared up into the nearly black orbs of a dark-complexioned, dark-haired man of India descent. I couldn't have guessed it from his accent, however, which had a decidedly destined-for-Oxford *flavour.*

"Jumpy, aren't we?" a woman stated. I hadn't see her, either, for she was dwarfed by the tall man. She didn't look much like Toto, but as that was the only other character's name I had, I penciled her in for that role.

"Too much caffeine," I admitted.

"Try some natural spring water. It does wonders for the constitution."

"No, thanks. There are still some vices I cling to. I don't suppose anyone could ever eradicate vice from human nature."

"You think not?" That was Dorothy's voice. I looked around but didn't see her. It was probably just as well, for it reminded me these kids were of the techno generation. Maybe they didn't indulge in caffeine but they knew every gizmo in the book. Which, in itself, is an addiction. Only, they didn't see it. No one ever does.

"Hi, Dorothy." I waved to the air. The others exchanged glances. "I'm ready whenever you are."

I heard her laugh.

"We must remember not to underestimate you."

"It works both ways. How 'bout you showing yourself, or taking me to headquarters so we get started?"

Suddenly, all my ideas were heaped at the feet of, "The Best Laid Plans." It was time to put up or shut up.

Or, almost.

"I want in on whatever you're doing. You have your reasons; I have mine. They needn't be mutually exclusive. I can use the bread and I wouldn't mind walking around with my head held up for a change. You want an end to your play – so you say. But you're not only budding playwrights. You want more than to see your names in lights. A lot more. So do I. So let's stop fooling around and get down to it."

"He's an American," I heard the Wizard whisper to the tall man, who was odds-on-favorite to be the Cowardly Lion.

"Bring him," Dorothy commanded. Then added, for my benefit, "You won't mind being blindfolded?"

"I assume that while you phrased that as a question, it's rhetorical? Of course I mind being blindfolded. Who wouldn't? But if it's the only way you trusting souls are gonna get on with this, then wrap the bandage around my eyes and let's get the show on the road."

The Wizard took a hood from his oversized pocket and fitted it over my face. It was like one of those Ninja masks the kids wear at Halloween, except that there were no eye holes. I heard snickering as the troupe admired their new player.

"I like him better like that," one declared.

"Yeah. He can play one of the Munchkins," the Lion quipped.

I felt more like Blind Justice but didn't say so.

One of them shoved me and I stumbled backwards, awkwardly regained my balance then shuffled ahead toward where I presumed the door to be. While I had a pretty good idea of the layout of the cafe, it was disconcerting to realize how soon one loses one's bearings when the lights are snuffed out.

Someone – the woman, I thought, from the size of her hand – took me by the arm and walked me out into the street. I was acutely aware of how cold it had become. A moment before, with both eyes open, I had dismissed the temperature, but now, deprived of that most useful ability to see, I had to rely on my other, less developed and until now, less appreciated senses.

I didn't question why I was more temperature sensitive. Technically, cold had nothing to do with vision, so it didn't make much sense. I just went with the flow.

We walked maybe one hundred yards, then I was turned around three times – the requisite number used in every novel since the dawn of fiction – and shoved into a car. My first idiotic thought was astonishment that they should have found a parking space so near the cafe, when Gypsy and I had parked light years away.

I was warming to my role as Themis.

It was a big vehicle, not a mini-van or a SUV, because the seats were padded and it smelled of leather and wood. That pegged it for an expensive car, a Rolls probably. I sniffed again, then laughed. I could sense their curiosity.

"What's the joke, mate?"

"I was remembering a story I covered on an otherwise dull news day," I began, listening to the gentle purr of the engine. "This luxury car dealer was receiving complaints from his customers that the top-of-the-line modes didn't feel right. They had lost some of the old *pizzazz*. No one liked them and they were returning them for their money back.

"The cars were sent back to the factory, where the engineers were baffled. The cars ran the same, sounded the same, looked the same. And then some bright boy realized the trouble. The manufacturer, in time-honored fashion, had substituted wood-grained plastic for the burl in the dash. You couldn't tell by eye that a substitution had taken place, but the new cars didn't *smell* like the old cars."

"So what did the manufacturer do? Go back to burl?" came the question, so innocently spoken I was taken aback for a moment.

"Of course not. He had some bozo in the lab make a burl-scented spray. As soon as a car was sold, they squirted in all over the dash and the new owner drove it away, happy as a clam."

I laughed. Alone, as it turned out.

I think I had offended their noble sensitivities.

Remembering the ritzy grammar school they had attended, I should have guessed.

We drove for about fifty minutes, which could have taken us around in circles or out of the city. I tried to identify sounds but the windows were rolled up and the motor was quite sound-proofed. If nothing else, that would have alerted me it wasn't a Ford.

It made me sad, though, to flunk my John Steed test. Remember the episode where he was blindfolded and taken out into the country? When he retraced his route later, he found the exact spot by remembering he had heard a flock of geese at the turnoff.

I didn't hear any geese.

Well, I'm not one for remakes, anyway. And I could never step into Patrick Macnee's bowler.

When the car stopped, I had just about been lulled into sleep. I jerked my head up, startled that I couldn't see anything, then remembered the blindfold. My first instinct was to take it off, which is exactly what I did. I think the others were drowsy themselves, because they didn't respond until it was too late.

"You shouldn't have done that, Dads," the Lion menacingly growled at me.

"Dude, mate, man, pal or Herman all work with me, but lose the 'Dads,'" I growled back. "Biologically I might just be old enough to be your sire, but I'm not and don't appreciate the familiarity."

"He thinks you're a nigger," the Wizard joked. I turned to him, seriously pissed.

"I don't like that word and I don't like being called 'Dads.' I never had a 'dad' of my own, and I'm not anyone's 'dad.' Don't patronize me; if I'm not on your side – if you didn't bring me here to help you – then do whatever it is you're going to do and be done with it."

My tone grew harsher.

"But I sure as hell hope you're not planning on holding me for ransom, because you're wasting your time. No one I know has ever sat in a Rolls Royce, let alone owned one," I said, pointing to the Winged Lady, "so they're not in your league, financially."

"Whoa," Dorothy commanded, putting a stop to the argument before it got really ugly. "No offense, Kimbo."

I turned to her, fast. She was smiling, the way a cobra ready to strike would look, if only it had lips. It cooled me down in a hurry.

"Sorry. I'm touchy on the subject. And I'm not a bigot," I darkly added. "Accuse me of being a bad writer and I'll stick a pen nub in your eye, but call me –"

"No one's calling you anything," she placated. "Least of all a bad writer. Hell," she teased, "we haven't read enough of your work to judge you."

I noted the "enough" and nodded. They, too, had done their homework.

"OK. Let's go and get some work done."

We were standing near the entranceway of a mansion, which looked to be a cross between the White House and Thornfield Hall. I followed Dorothy as she led the way up the steps and to the front door. I expected her to use an old-fashioned door knocker and have a butler in livery answer the massive double doors, but she turned the knob herself and admitted us.

She went in first, followed by the Wizard, then me. The others trailed behind. A light burned in the foyer but that was the only illumination I could see. When she plunged into the darkness beyond, I followed. It wasn't until we were all inside the study and the door shut behind, that someone turned on a desk lamp and I got a decent look around the room.

By American standards, it was large enough to be an efficiency apartment. If anyone spoke above a whisper, I expected the words would echo off the walls. A mammoth desk was situated by the windows, immediately to my right. The floor-length curtains were drawn, but I imagined the outside glass ran from ground to ceiling.

A leather chair was pulled up to the desk and might have done service as a throne for Henry VII. On the desk was a blotter, a mahogany stationary box, a matching pen holder with half a dozen Waterman fountain pens, a wooden in-basket, a pipe rack with four Dunhill White Dot estate-quality pipes, and a humidor. (I've been told it isn't "white dot" but "white spot," yet I can't get over the image which looks like a dot rather than a spot, in case you're keeping score of my mistakes.)

Four leather chairs were placed a comfortable distance from the desk, while a reading chair was set apart, nearer the windows. Wall-to-wall, built-in bookcases with glass, lawyer's-style doors to protect the weighty tomes, lined the other three walls. It was the kind of room I would design when I won the lottery.

Forgetting myself for the moment, I crossed to the nearest book case, pulled up the heavy leaded glass door and withdrew a book. It was a first edition of *The Man Who Laughed,* printed on glossy paper and filled with hand-colored woodcuts. If I had ever known envy, this was it.

Reverently replacing the book, I wandered to the desk and picked up the perfectly balanced fountain pen. It might have been crafted to fit my hand. With such an instrument, a writer who had already created his one masterpiece with a number-one pencil on college-ruled notebook paper, could wile away his days writing drivel, while wondering where his creativity went.

A paradox, but one in which I was willing to submit.

I handled the pipes, next, my mouth watering. Given a month, I could easily have my teeth marks imprinted into the stems, so that when I smoked, the pipe would rest comfortably in my mouth.

"Go ahead. Sit in the chair," Dorothy suggested. I didn't ask for a second invitation.

The chair was a bit too large for me and lower to the ground than suited my frame, but that was easily rectified. Relaxing back into the comfortable, shoulder-high back, I signed hedonistically and surveyed my kingdom.

It was only then that I realized the missing item. Or, rather, items. There was no high tech equipment of any sort. Not even a typewriter. I stared quizzically across at my hosts.

"Nice digs. But where's the techno-gizmos?"

Dorothy gave a signal and the boys scurried to unearth the laptop they had stashed under the desk. In a moment, the familiar hum of the motor-driven device filled my ears. In such a room, it was out of place and alien. While I've never been one to resent technology, I would have tossed it through the window at that moment and replace it with a peck-and-pound manual.

Dorothy sat in one of the leather chairs, crossed her legs and held court.

"You said you are one of us."

"Want to see my tattoos?" I stupidly inquired.

"Perhaps," she stated in so matter-of-fact a voice I blushed and wished I was somewhere else. "At the moment, I want you to speak of world power."

"There are those who have it and those who want it. I'm in the latter group."

"How do we know that?"

Good question.

I pondered, weak and weary.

"I know you people are into something – unique. I started out investigating a simple power outage and discovered it was anything but the Modern Curse. The deed was perpetrated by a group calling themselves Auntie EM – the E. M. standing for electromagnetic power. The 'Auntie' being a play on words from the *Wizard of Oz.*

"You're Dorothy, otherwise known as Eleanor Andress. James Polle is the Wizard. The others, I'm guessing, are Timothy Button-Rhoades, Paul Wiedenmyer. My friend there is Noel Delaney, the Lion. (I judiciously omitted the descriptive "Cowardly.") And Mary Keswick, there, is Toto."

There was a stunned silence before one of the boys – it was too dark in the room to see much past the arc of light from the desk lamp – swore softly. Almost reverently. It spoke of a good Church of England upbringing.

"How the fuck did you find out all that?" he asked, after clearing his throat, in lieu of rinsing his mouth with holy water.

"I told you – I'm a reporter. It's my business to ferret out details thought to be coincidence by the authorities. I'm good at what I do. Too good for my own good, if you know what I mean. When I caught onto what you were doing –"

"Exactly what *are* we doing?" the Wizard interrupted.

"Using technology to disrupt civilization. Blocking power sources with EM. Nothing serious – a grammar school heating system; all the lights on Theatre Row; the phones and traffic signals in a yuppy neighborhood. Tests, weren't they? Or, rather, threats? You went to the cops – Scotland Yard – and told them what you were going to do.

"And then you made good your threats. It's all very simple, isn't it? You can carry your jamming device in a briefcase. Turn it on, and bingo! Off go the lights. Away goes two hundred years of technology with the simple turn of a dial. Bloodless warfare. Who needs atom bombs and land mines when you can take an entire city with one flick of a switch?"

I waited for the classic, ever popular, "He knows too much to live," line.

I wasn't disappointed.

Good writers aren't made, they're born.

"He's a spy! The bastard's from the Yard!"

That from Toto, of all "people."

"Hardly," I demurred. "I'm not here to arrest you. I'm here to join in on the fun. I want in."

"He's bugged," either the Scarecrow or the Tin Man cried. "Search him."

I hadn't counted on that. Before I could – euphemistically – defend myself, two of the boys grabbed me up out of my comfortable chair and ripped the clothes off my back. When I was down to my skivvies, I shouted protest.

"Enough, already!"

They stared at me in a very peculiar fashion. Being a male of my generation, I immediately dropped my hands to my jock, thinking my sexual ability was being appraised. This time, I was wrong.

Hollywood would never forgive these wannabes.

They were ogling my "tattoos."

"Jesus, will you look at him!" one of them exclaimed. I thought he was going to finish with, "He looks like a freak out of the circus!" but erred on the side of conventionalism. "Where'd you get those done?"

"A friend did it for me," I responded, truthfully, as it happened. "She's very good with a – she has an artist's eye."

They crowded around me, one of the group tilting the banker's lamp just enough to cast a greenish light over my body.

"What's this?" Toto asked, pointing to a figure on my tummy.

"It's a Gypsy symbol for power," I admitted, hearing Gypsy's words as she explained it to me while engraving it on my skin. "It has something to do with strength and becoming one with nature."

In fact, the complex arrangement of lightning, clouds, mountains and cuneiform letters was a depiction of an ancient Gypsy blessing. I thought it wouldn't be stretching the description to add "power" to the list.

"How long have you had these?"

"Since I came to England and discovered a new way of looking at the world."

That sounded better than "several hours."

The coterie pawed over me, making low, inarticulate sounds of approval. The only one who remained seated was Dorothy, although she never took her eyes off me. My face, that is. I guessed she wasn't the comic book type.

"So." It was Dorothy who finally broke up the admiration society. "You have done well, Mister Kimbo. Very well. I am impressed."

I knew a left-handed compliment when I heard one.

"I'm tired of hacking my life away, making peanuts. I've been in the Big Time and I've been in the Dumps enough to know which I like better," I stated with utter un-emotion. "I learned to play the Game; just like you learned. I'm a dumb reporter and you're just grammar school graduates. I'm a nice man and you're nice kids. But, we both know better."

I said "both," rather than "all," speaking directly, one-on-one, to her. It was her show. She was, after all, the star.

The power with the briefcase.

The author of the fantasy.

"So," she repeated. "You want in."

"I want in."

"We have no character left for you to play. They have all been taken."

I remembered what Gypsy had said about their play-acting and thought fast.

There is one part you haven't filled," I pointed out.

"That being?"

"Auntie Em. Small 'm,'" I hastened to add.

There was a long moment of silence. Long in lifetimes, fast in time.

"You're right," she admitted. "We did wonder about that omission."

I breathed a sigh of relief. I was "in."

That was a running gag from an old Boris Karloff movie, spoken by a character called Petty Louie.

He kept trying to get "in" on Boris' invention of a "night key," which opened the locks of all the jewelry stores.

As I remembered, the film had a happy ending for everyone but Petty Louie, who ended up "buying the farm."

I was "in." Now I hoped I wouldn't end up being buried underneath it.

ACT 13

"What is this place, anyway?" I dared ask as the dust settled. I figured that if I were truly "in," I ought to know something about their hideout.

It was Second-Billed "Joe" who filled me in.

"We're renting it."

The rest (omitting Dorothy, obviously) giggled.

"I get it. It's not one of your ancestral castles. The owners went away on extended holiday and you picked the lock. Nice idea. But where's the caretaker, or the dutiful houseful of servants? Tied up in closets?"

"Nothing so cliché as that, Auntie," Dorothy answered. "In these days of cost-cutting and mandatory time-off for the help, it's all arranged so they're gone when the masters are away. The house is left in charge of a solicitor, who contracted his responsibility out to a group of students – who incidentally agreed to maintain the grounds, polish the silver and dust the furniture."

"You didn't even have to break in!" I exclaimed, gushing with approval. Some of it was stage frills, but the rest was sincere. It was a neat trick.

"And the Rolls? You take it for a walk every evening so it doesn't spring an oil leak in the garage?"

"I like that," the Tin Man exclaimed. "We'll have to save that line for our next play."

"Help yourself," I graciously permitted. "Now: down to brass tacks. What do you want me to do, and can I have my clothes back?"

"In that order?" Toto teased. It was hardly a solicitation, but I blushed anyway.

"It wouldn't do to have Auntie Em running around in her unmentionables," I pointed out. "And it wouldn't have passed the 1939 sensors, either."

"It's a new century," Dorothy countered, making me sorry I had overwritten my part. The Cowardly Lion went to toss me my pants when she stopped him. "I think not. Proper or no, he's safer the way he is. For now," she added, giving me some, but not much, hope.

Before I could think of an appropriate "thank you," we all heard a slight rustling outside the window. The blood froze in my veins, thinking it was the local authorities, comes to haul us all off to jail. Sweet might be convinced to bail me out on a breaking and entering change, but if a rival rag ever got a picture of me dressed – err, undressed – like this, it would be the end of my illustrious career.

"See what that is," Dorothy commanded. The Scarecrow went to the curtain, drew it back and peered out.

"It's the cat," he exclaimed. I don't know about the others, but I left out a sigh of relief.

"Then feed the damned thing in the kitchen and lock it in. I thought you told me you had gotten rid of it," Dorothy added with a decidedly sour tone.

"I did," Scarecrow murmured. "It must have come back. Cats have nine lives, you know."

His statement left a bitter taste in my mouth. I've been reduced to the status of an alley cat a time or two in my life, and didn't appreciate people "getting rid" of ferals. And the way she delivered her line reminded me of Allister Sim in *Scrooge*. Something about decreasing the excess population.

Scarecrow disappeared. We all waited for his return, as though the play could not go on without all its players.

In a moment there was a thud, like the flat of a shovel hitting bone, followed by a high pitched scream, a brief scuffle, then silence. When he returned, no one asked him if he had left out the cream.

"All right. Let's get to work," Dorothy ordered. "The play is the thing. Auntie," she continued, turning to me. "We've already reviewed Acts One through Three. This is a Four act work."

"Like a television programme," I quipped.

"We do not watch the telly," I was informed. "This is serious drama."

"Is that why you closed down the play houses on Theatre Row? No one would accept your production?"

I hit close to home. There was an uncomfortable silence. The kind one hears before the warden throws the switch.

"Act One was at the school," Dorothy continued, letting my *faux pas* go. It started out as a rehearsal but when one-of-us," she emphasized, looking at the Wizard, "would have been disqualified from performing, had he failed his term exams, we thought it better to open without final preparations. It worked splendidly."

I nodded, mentally thanking her for confirming Gypsy and my suspicions.

"Act Two was at Theatre Row. We saw no reason why the 'legitimate theatre' should be allowed to go on, when our play had been so summarily rejected."

I nodded again. Once more, and I'd need suction cups to stick myself to the back of a car windscreen.

"Another unqualified success." She smiled this time. "We made all the papers. You covered that story, perhaps?"

"No. I'm a crime reporter." I sniffed. "No one was hurt. But," I added quickly, sensing her displeasure, "I did have a friend who missed out on watching a play. She got her two hundred pounds back, but was sorely disappointed. Quite a ruckus, as I understand."

"It was meant as a warning: the Theatre is dead. That was the first time we notified Scotland Yard. We did not ask for much. We received nothing."

In the pending silence no one applauded.

"Act Three, was the power outage across an entire London district. That made them stand up and pay attention."

A decided smirk.

"But not enough. Our… demands were too high. So be it. Now, we take what we want."

"What, exactly, is it you want?" I asked.

"Respect. Acknowledgment of our artistic genius. Power. We want to rule, Auntie. In our previous Acts, we learned the Establishment has no room for experimental theatre. It wants nothing more than for things to go on as they always have. Dull routine. The same tired actors repeating the same worn-out lines. We're the new wave. The Next Generation."

I felt like Captain Kirk, trapped in a not-so-parallel Universe, watching strange life forms operate his beloved *Enterprise.*

I told you I wasn't much for remakes. If I could have stopped that one, I would have, but no one asked me. *Auntie Em, The Next Generation* was mine to script. For the first time, I salivated. It was a Trekkers dream come true. Return rightful command of the starship to Jim and Spock and Bones.

Maybe Queen Elizabeth and Tony Blair and the daily commuters of Planet London weren't exactly the crew of NCC-1701, but this was as close to Hollywood as I was ever going to get.

"And Act Four?" I prompted.

"Act Four has yet to be written. That's where you come in."

That was my cue, if ever I heard one.

I Winked an Eye.

"I'm ready."

"There is the computer. Write."

I moved my command chair into position, fingers hovering over the keys. The Klieg Lights came on. The Camera dollied in for a Close Up. The Action commenced with...

FADE IN:

INT. MANSION - ESTABLISHING SHOT – NIGHT

Waves of energy, pulsating across the screen. Everything is BLURRY, INDISTINCT.

Faint HUMMING of equipment. TENSION in the air.

CLOSE UP – BRIEFCASE

Simple, unadorned, <u>faux </u>leather; the type carried by countless businessmen,
tourists and IRA splinter groups. HOLD, then CAMERA PULLS BACK to reveal
London. It is DAY. A busy morning.

> DOROTHY'S VOICE
> (calm; in command)
> Throw the switch. And let what has been
> perish.

FULL SHOT - THE AUNTIE EM GROUP – DAY

Dorothy stands in FOREGROUND, the Wizard to her side. Behind them are the
Scarecrow, the Tin Man, the Cowardly Lion, Toto and Auntie Em. All are in costume
from <u>The Wizard of Oz.</u> No one pays them the slightest attention. This is London,
after all, where the odd is the commonplace. There is a SLIGHT AURA around
them.

CLOSER ANGLE - DOROTHY AND WIZARD

as the Wizard opens the briefcase. Inside is a mass of super-techno gadgetry. He
depresses several buttons. Lights come ON; a LOW HUMMING of power.
HOLD, then CAMERA PULLS BACK TO REVEAL:

WIDE ANGLE - LONDON – DAY

Suddenly, all the mechanical lights go OUT. No traffic lights, no neon. Motor

vehicles won't start; those waited at traffic lights are CRASHED into from those behind them.

In the b.g., someone SCREAMS.

"This is it!" the Tin Man cheered. "Act Four!"

Destruction was in the air. The little group and I, armed with our new, Modern Technology, possessed of an electro-magnet field powerful enough to bring down a low-flying plane, had put Act Four into action. Inspired by my vision of mass destruction and a city crippled by a total loss of anything electric or battery-driven; psyched by my descriptions of a government acknowledging their demands for total capitulation, Dorothy, Wizard, Tim Man, Scarecrow, Cowardly Lion, Toto and Auntie Em had turned fantasy into reality.

With the group leaning over the desk, or standing behind me, they hung on every word I wrote. Before their eyes, I typed like a Mad Thing, intoxicated by their desires. And not incidentally, their praise.

"That's it, mate!"

"You're a genius, Auntie!"

"Shakespeare and Hitler, thrown into one!"

On an ego trip of my own, I wrote what I imagined would happen if Auntie EM did everything it was supposed to. I made them Rulers of the Universe; set up scenes with them escaping pursuit. Described the authorities as hapless clowns. God help me, I ever typed a subplot of them receiving OBE's and Orders of the Garter before being crowned Queens and Kings.

On paper, it was all so simple, so easy, so foolproof. As the last words, depicting them cheering in celebration of their triumph over the words FADE OUT, were typed, the SCENE RETURNED TO REALITY.

Just as I had written, the Thespians from Hell were cheering, replaying their triumph in their mind's eyes. Damn the torpedoes and full speed ahead for the play no one wanted to buy. Off-Off Broadway had triumphed over the Great White Way.

I cheered with my companions, they being none the wiser that I rah-rahed an octave lower than they. Me – a reporter and would-be novelist – had set the stage for the greatest world tragedy since Hiroshima.

What had gone wrong? What had happened to my plan to save the world? I was supposed to prevent the very scenario which I had just perpetrated.

Something had transformed me, turned me into a world destroyer rather than a world saver. I had betrayed my conscience, just as these kids had done, in exchange for the ultimate thrill of seeing my name in lights.

But the lights had all gone out.

Some one or some thing had activated Auntie EM.

I tried to remember exactly what transpired, but it was a mass of confusion. I had been sitting there, at the laptop, composing Act Four of *Auntie EM,* the play. I meant to scramble the plot, type in a Fatal Flaw, set these would-be World Thespians up for capture, then return to the CANS Building and really write myself one hell of a headline.

Instead, I had been swallowed up by my character, by the idea of success. I had scripted the Devil's Masterpiece, a world take-over. My words were no longer fiction, but fact.

My first instinct was the return to the computer and rewrite the ending. Have them get caught. Bring in Scotland Yard like knights in shining armor. Reverse the destruction. My hands draped over the keyboard and I made a gallant effort to type. Nothing happened. And then, too late, I realized why. The power had gone off. The *electric* typewriter had ceased to function.

Like it or not, I was one of them now.

All the world's a stage....

A scream came out on nowhere. In the darkness, I couldn't be certain who was in trouble, but he was close. Maybe five feet close. My eyes riveted around the room, trying to identify objects, put things into perspective, all the while fascinated by the horror unfolding. My mind, a mass of conflicting emotions, idiotically thought, *"Dial 911."* It only took me a moment to remember, that, One: I wasn't in the States, and Two: none of the phones worked.

I took a step, two steps, then stumbled into a body without the least idea what was wrong with him or how to help. As my eyes adjusted to the gloom I could just make out the Scarecrow's face had turned a ghastly shade of blue as he clutched at his heart.

"What's the matter?" I screamed to be heard over the din. Not his, incidentally, for by this time, he had stopped making any noise at all.

He stared at me, eyes popping out of his head. I'm sure you've probably heard, and certainly read that trite expression: eyes popping out of his head. And probably dismissed it, as I had done. But believe me: this man's eyes were literally protruding from his skull. Had they shot out and rolled toward me, I would have bent over to pick them up, convinced they were marbles.

He Stoops To Conquer.

I no longer wanted to conquer; I just wanted to get the hell out of this disaster. Yet, in my twisted moral agony, I felt I had an obligation to this stranger.

"Are you having a heart attack?"

I wasn't sure he could answer me, or even understand what I was saying. When he made an attempt to communicate, I put my ear next to his lips.

"Something's wrong," Scarecrow gasped with his dying breath. "I think... my pacemaker stopped working. I need it to...."

What he needed became a moot point as he decompressed like a deflated balloon, crumpled and seemingly became half the size he had been in life.

Death was like that: it reduced a body to its lowest common denominator.

It occurred to me that I ought to perform CPR on him. I had taken a class once, several years ago when Sweet was on a "Save a Life" kick. He got like that every once in a while. No one ever knew what triggered it or how long it would last. Once he had been bitten with the "Exercise for Fitness" program, and we all did jumping jacks in the office. That ended when his dietitian told him jelly doughnuts were *verboten,* no matter how much exercise he took.

My mind ran over those silly acronyms you're forced to memorize. RACE came to mind. Now, what did it stand for?

Ram your fist into their heart area.
Aim your lips toward their mouth.
Compress the chest.
Enquire about insurance and ask if the state you're in has Good Samaritan Laws.

And what was that ratio of air puffs to chest compressions? 2:10? 1:5? 50-100?

Who could remember at a time like this?

If the guy had a pacemaker, would I knock it out of place by hitting him in the sternum? If I could get him to my car, maybe I could hook him up to the jumper cables and jump start the damned thing.

Then it came to me, like going over Niagara Falls in a barrel. Pacemaker. Runs on a battery. Auntie Em had stopped all the electrical devices and batteries from working. No computers, no lights, no phones, no watches. No pacemakers.

I cried, put a hand to my own heart and staggered backward, nearly knocking the Cowardly Lion off his feet.

"What's the matter with you, mate?" he demanded. "You getting drunk on all this?"

"That man," I pointed. "He has a pacemaker which generates the electricity to make his heart pump. Auntie EM turned it off. We just murdered him!"

The Lion shrugged and moved away. He could not comprehend what I was saying.

Or didn't want to.

Furious, I reached behind him, grasped hold of his shoulder and pulled him around.

"We just killed that man. Look at him. He's dead. By turning off the juice, his heart stopped beating."

For a moment his eyes cleared and I saw Noel Delaney come back.

"I never thought about that," he hesitantly admitted. "Why the hell didn't he tell us he had a pacemaker?"

"And more to the point," Dorothy deadpanned, "why didn't it kill him before?"

Opting to believe she was concerned, rather than coolly dispassionate, I blurted, "He must not have been in the radius of the electromagnetic field."

"That's right," Toto agreed. "None of us were around. We just left the suitcase and got away before the fun started."

Now clear-headed and sick, I cringed at her word choice before shouting, "Turn Auntie EM off. Maybe it's not too late!"

"This is the Bloodless Revolution, baby," Dorothy interjected, thus rending my optimism moot. "This is what it's all about. We're on the verge of a complete takeover!"

Cowardly Lion nodded agreement and I saw I had lost him. They were in it too deeply, had imagined this day too long to be drawn back by proofs positive.

"You crazy lunatics," I shouted.

My words were drowned out by the sound of Dorothy giving orders.

Come on! The party's starting without us!"

Kicking aside the dead body of one of their own – or, rather, one who had written himself out of a co-starring role, she indicated everyone make a mad dash for the Rolls. I immediately saw this as my chance for a getaway, but somehow I couldn't bring myself to escape. I belonged to them, now. The Wizard had imbibed the scenes I had written and turned on Auntie EM. Not using the pittance of power they had employed in their trial runs, but the Big Time.

I had made it real and now they wanted to savor their victory. Like it or not, I had to go with them. We all crammed into the car, Dorothy at the helm of our flying ship. I imagined we'd go down the driveway, through the back roads and toward the city. A city that had found itself plunged into darkness. Before I realized the car wouldn't start. We got out and started running.

Through the hyperspace created by the magnetism, we reached London proper in no time flat. Needless to say, traffic lights didn't work. We had already established that little parlor trick. Neon, electric lamps, phones: all dead. Running like things possessed, we veered in and out of traffic, occasionally crisscrossing medians or the shoulders to get ahead of those who had panicked and come to a… dead stop. Nearly smacking a man standing in the middle of the expressway waving his hands to warn of stalled vehicles ahead, the Wizard laughed. The sound chilled me to the bone.

This wasn't a bloodless revolution. It was everyone for himself, and those who survived the crash of civilization were willing and able to assume the leadership of a black and white world. London had become Kansas without knowing why.

The closer we got to the city, the worse the damage. People stranded at the top of high-rises were leaning out windows screaming for help. People trapped in elevators (I presumed) were crossing themselves and praying for the power to return before their bladders burst. Or, the power came back on and they were plunged 22 floors to the underground parking. Lacking phones, bystanders were shouting at one another, the first time in their lives they had ever spoken to another human being face-to-face. I imagined Sweet ordering his electric typewriter to turn on so he could write an editorial the wire services couldn't print.

Perhaps more eerie than anything else was the silence. Aside from the screams, that is, no music blared from open café doors; no personal headsets filled the minds of the Great Unwashed with radio talk shows that issued drivel catering to the paranoid audiences who listened to hosts repeating only those opinions their audience wanted to hear.

"Go! Go! Go!" Dorothy encouraged, inebriated with the idea of unlimited power.

One vehicle still working sideswiped a lorry, careened into the wrong lane (have I mentioned the British drive on the wrong side of the road? It has to do with gauge and the breadth of wagon wheels) and blew a tire. The truck burst into flame. The Tin Man cursed in horror and Dorothy shot him a look that would kill. The Cowardly Lion threw up his guts.

Hurrying to the lorry, I jerked up the handle, pulled open and door and grabbed the driver. Naturally, I had entered the vehicle from the wrong side, so I had to yank him across the seat. Fortunately, he wasn't wearing a seatbelt or had already unhooked it. My effort and his weight caused us to fall backward, he landing on top of me. Wiggling out from underneath him, I grabbed his head and stared into his face.

"You OK?" I harshly demanded.

"What happened?" When it was obvious I wasn't going to answer, he swore, then politely added, "Thanks, gov. You saved my life."

Shamed by being thanked for an event I had started, I backed away, hands help up.

"Get to the side of the road and stay there. Help is on the way."

He began to shake. I didn't want to believe it was because he knew I was lying.

Scrambling to my feet, my attention was drawn to a loud crash. Along with my fellow destructionists I looked in the direction of the noise, witnessing a ten-car pileup at the intersection. A moment later several more cars roared into those already too crippled to get out of the way. From the voracity of the impact, I didn't have to wonder if anyone had died.

Wonder was a thing of the past. Death was all around us, like the Black Plague.

Spread by the Rats from Oz.

There was only one thing to do: try and get my hands on the Briefcase and smash it to smithereens. Hardly moved to empathy, the Wizard was clutching it, demonically pointing it to the four winds, as though it were some carved figurine, either meant to bring rain, or to shower evil on the heads of an invading enemy.

I circled around the car hoping to grab it from him but the Tin Man divined my purpose. He shoved out his leg just before I sped past, catching me full force. I hit it, bounced off, picked myself up and lunged at him. He hadn't expected the turnaround, enabling me to grab him by the shoulders and yank him to the ground. Lacking anything more substantial, I hit him with my head, somewhere between his ribs and belt. I felt the gush of air expel from his lungs as we both went down.

Never having time or opportunity for games as a child, I fell poorly, nearly wrenching my right arm out of its socket. My fingers went numb. Undeterred, I began pounding him with my good left hand, pummeling him with blows. I didn't care where I hit him. Anywhere would suffice.

I ended up doing him more damage with my knee, which jerked spasmodically into his groin. He cried out and rolled away from me, clutching his Big Hurt, cursing and damning me for hitting below the belt. All right, it wasn't cricket, but I was an American and could plead innocent of knowing the rules.

In my present state of mind, I might have finished him off, right then and there, but he wasn't my target. I needed to stop the Wizard with his magic box. Scrambling to my feet, I stated wildly around myself, trying to locate him. He was nowhere in sight.

As long as we were playing games, I shouted the first thing which came to mind.

"All-e, all-e, all-e in-free! Come out, come out, wherever you are!"

I guess they didn't play hide and seek in the U.K. for no one took advantage of my offer.

I tried a more basic approach.

"Look for the Wizard of Oz. Grab the guy with the briefcase! He's the one doing all this"

Admittedly, I wasn't in my right mind. Those people foolish enough to believe me turned their heads one way, then the other, identifying any and all with bags, packages, books, purses, or any item remotely similar to a briefcase. In the panic, they jumped innocent pedestrians, regardless of gender, beating them to an inch of their lives, then stomping on their discarded possessions.

No one found the right perpetrator, however, for the lights did not come back on. What happened, instead, was a general melee, with fists flying everywhere. Instead of helping my cause, I had made it one thousand times worse.

With a sob of misery, I pulled one man off the body of a prostrate woman, helped her up, then dragged her into an alley. For my trouble, she belted me a good one across my face. I staggered back, muttered an apology for saving her life, and dragged myself away.

"Think," I ordered myself.

I might as well have ordered the world to stop revolving, for the response I got. My brain was well past thinking. It wanted only to get out, escape from the mass destruction of a powerless world.

There was really no place for me to go. I knew that. I was the author of all this, after all. I had written Act Four too well. I had placed into operation too many foolproof methods of preservation.

And chuckled while I was creating it.

Which proved one thing.

Never underestimate the might of the pen. Even if you use a typewriter or a laptop, rather than a Flair or a #1 pencil. They all worked the same.

ACT 14

Chaos, chaos, chaos everywhere.

Given time, I could think of a rhyme for that little ditty and make myself a poet.

On second thought, never mind. I didn't want to be a poet, a screenwriter, a novelist, *or* a playwright. I didn't want anything at all to do with writing.

All I wanted to do was crawl into a hole and die.

But I couldn't. All the holes were already occupied by dead bodies.

In lieu of the ultimate escape, no reservations needed, I thought about running. Remember that old series, *Run For Your Life,* with Ben Gazarra? He played a wealthy (they're always wealthy) something or other (a lawyer?) with a soon-to-be fatal disease. The series where they refused to film an ending because they were afraid of ruining their syndication sales? I could sympathize. I wanted to run and run and run. Out of London. Out of England.

Maybe as far away as Wales. Or Whales, if I swam too far. It didn't matter. I just needed to get away, to have time to think this whole thing through.

But I couldn't. Call it a conscious. A Moral Responsibility.

Fancy words to explain a simple concept.

Guilt.

A bunch of crazy kids had appealed to my vanity. They asked me to pen a chapter- to-end-all-chapters: to write Act Four for *Auntie EM.* I had done so and those lunatics had acted it out, just the way I wrote it.

Crawling into an abandoned boutique the looters had already hit, I situated myself under a table and sat, elbows resting on knees, hands supporting chin.

What to do?

The Sixty-Four Thousand Dollar Question.

"That was the Olde Days," I grunted to myself. "We're up to one million dollars, now." I was the *Survivor*. Only I didn't want to be. Not like this.

Somehow, I had to stop what I had scripted.

Going to Scotland Yard was useless. The only hope they had was to find the Oz Gang, throw them behind bars and destroy their all-powerful briefcase gizmo. However, I knew M-16 couldn't find them. I had written a dozen contingency plans for the Ozites and even I didn't know which ones they'd use, or in what order. If I put "Rocket Scientist" onto them, gave him the true identities and play names of Eleanor, James, Timothy, Paul, Noel and Mary, what could he do? All these kids had to do was take a bath, cut (or grow) their hair, put on business attire, and paint long faces on their otherwise jubilant countenances.

Dressed like working adults, they'd blend in anywhere. Never mind fingerprints, or whatever it is they do in criminal investigations today. These maniacs were intelligent and in possession of a weapon so powerful it could wipe out the power of an entire city while resting inconspicuously in a two-handled shopping bag from Harrods.

They were also in possession of my grammatically-correct way to demand blackmail. With time and EM on their side, they'd make their demands and have things pretty much their own way.

I thought about the Gypsy. I had lost track of her just before going into that GM-Free Zone and meeting my fate. I didn't know whether she had been able to follow me to the mansion, but doubted it. First, she didn't have a car. Second, if she *had* followed me, she surely would have divined what I was doing and tried to out put a stop to it.

So: where was she? And would she ever speak to me again, knowing I had joined the Other Side? I didn't even know how to contact her. All the phones were dead ducks. None of the cabs were running – for any price – and the double-deckers were also out of commission. In any case, the streets were so congested, I couldn't get through in a Yugo.

Walking all the way to her place was out of the question. My bum knee was acting up and I doubted I could make the three or four kilometers to her pad. She might not even be there. Clearly, she lived in close enough proximity to the EM device to have experienced a total blackout. She would have divined I failed in my mission to stop the dastardly deeds of the Oz Gang.

I could only hope she wouldn't know how intricate my own role had been in pulling off their coup. But, of course, she could read my mind, if not my face. How explain to a White Knight, the well-meaning Don Quixote had joined the evil Windmills?

I heard a noise in the doorway and shivered. My hiding place would not be safe for long. While the boutique had already been looted once, there were still plenty of perfume bottles to smash and negligees to steal. When the mob got bored stuffing their faces on bagels and trying on gold chains from one of the many jewelry stores along the boulevard, they'd be back.

Getting gingerly to my feet, I staggered, more from the weight of guilt, than my macaroni knee, glanced around for a back exit, then picked my way over the broken glass and multitude of wigs and cashmere shawls. At the rear was a door. A pre-printed written sign proclaimed, "Emergency Exit. Warning Bells Will Sound if this Door is Opened During Regular Business Hours."

I didn't know what time it was because my watch had stopped. And anyway, I figured it didn't matter. It *was* an emergency. Also, there was no juice to sound an alarm.

I tried the door handle and it didn't budge. In my best imitation of countless cowboy heroes, I put my shoulder to the door and banged it. But no clever, underpaid screen writer had scripted my escape, and the door remained as intact as the Rock of Gibraltar.

Cursing unkind things about Saturday matinees, I scanned the rear of the shop, found a window (unbroken, wouldn't you know?) and threw a wooden head, looking naked and decapitated without its human hairdo and hat, through the glass. I cringed a moment from habit, fearing those dreaded alarm bells, then heaved a sigh of relief at the total silence my crime occasioned.

Going through a window is never as easy as you see on the telly. Usually the hero puts his head and shoulders through the Very Large Opening, then the director cuts to a new angle, and you see the hero on the other side, just pulling his leg out. Modern miracles.

It took me more than a few minutes to shove head, shoulders, torso and rump through the Very Small Opening I had made. Unfortunately, the glass chards in my window were real, not a thin sugar-film covering, and I cut my hands and sundry other parts of my anatomy wiggling out. Anyone could have told you, red-haired, freckled- faced, character-actor types never get cast as bigger-than-life, save-the-girl-from-the-railroad-tracks stars.

Once outside, I discovered the melee was progressing nicely. There were hundreds of people streaming everywhere, totally out of their heads. Without transportation, lights, sirens or electricity of any kind, the veneer of civilization had been wiped away. With one hundred years of inventions meant to speed-up life rendered useless, life hadn't been reduced to a crawl, it had mutated human beings into jack rabbits, running hither and yon, utterly purposeless.

Men ran head-long into women without excusing themselves (arguably a lost trait even before electricity); men slashed away with "brawleys," for the sheer savagery of having all the rules suspended; kicked those lying across their paths in their frenzy to enter a store, cross a street, or pick a pocket; women threw "mobiles" at one another, used over-sized pocketbooks as weapons, and made good cases for themselves as stunt men by hurtling through plate glass windows.

I saw no uniformed police, recognized no good Samaritans helping the wounded, the elderly and the very young. London was a place gone mad. Someone had opened the doors of Bedlam and the escapees had infected the entire population. This disease, brought on by a total freedom from electricity, affected everyone equally.

It was an across-the-boards free-for-all. Men dressed in top coats and bowlers, or baggy trousers and jackets with leather patches on the elbows; women in furs or Safeway's sale blouses and stretch slacks; kids wearing pure wool cardigans from Prohibito's and hair slicked back with gel, fought and grappled with those who "slept rough," all vying for prizes they could never – would never – use.

Without electricity or morality, London had transformed instantly from the modern-day capital of fashion and cuisine into a gigantic flea market where everything was marked "Free For the Taking."

I have often heard it said that one curse of the Industrial Revolution was noise pollution. The roar of motors, the shriek of horns, the hum of air conditioners, the ringing of phones, blare of boom boxes and rat-a-tat tats of construction workers, were all driving us crazy in ways we didn't understand. To go back to the Days of Yore, when the only noises were neighing of horses, squeals of unlubricated wagon wheels and street peddlers hawking their wares was to be desired.

Don't believe it. As I stood in the middle of the street devoid of mechanical pollution, I heard plenty of other, far more insidious sounds. Shouts, screams, curses; breaking glass. Moans from the injured, death rattles from the dying. What I wouldn't have given for the good, old-fashioned, comforting sound of a jack hammer.

Picking my way over prostrate bodies and streets strewn with high price-tagged instant junk, I crossed one thoroughfare, then started down a smaller one, known in the vernacular as a "rat run," without any clear plan in mind. There was nowhere to escape. The EM the Oz Gang had unleased on London had an effective range of fifty miles (mentioned in Act Three), far and away enough to blanket a city, 29 miles from north to south, 36 miles from west to east.

What I needed was some direction. Not necessarily map-wise, but plan wise. I had to clear my head, decide on a course of action. I might not have succeeded, had I not seen it. A bicycle.

With eyes alight with joy, I scrambled over sundry discarded items, leapt a bevy of tangled arms and legs and narrowly avoided a cache of paraphernalia, left, undoubtedly, when the seller – or user – found other ways to get dead.

The bike was chained to the curbside ring. This might have presented a problem for the ordinary thief, but not Yours Truly. While not a robber by inclination, I had "borrowed" on occasion in my life – usually, though not always – in times of dire need. My need now, was immediate and I didn't think twice about removing the small handy-dandy burglar's best friend from deep within my pants pocket. Snapping open the wire cutters, I freed the bike from its captivity and felt the liberator for doing so.

Swinging my leg over the bar, I settled my derriere into the ungodly uncomfortable seat, shifted my weight in accordance with the balance of the wheels, then peddled like a bat out of hell.

Freedom is a wonderful thing. My bike repaid me for cutting its tether by nearly throwing me at first "calming" I hit. In the States, such devices are called "speed bumps." They are supposed to slow down speeders. All I've ever known them to do is give the high-fliers a thrill.

Throwing out my legs, I steadied myself against the close-fitting brick walls, then continued on my journey, not any less reckless, but a bit more wary. Emerging from the alley, I took my bearings and peddled off in what I approximated to be the right direction.

The sights were all the same, whether I wheeled down main streets, or cut through the narrow sideways. People were out in force, most with glazed, blank, uncomprehending stares. The others – those who thrived on the knowledge that whatever crimes they perpetrated would go unpunished – took advantage of the rest. I saw boys steal purses from women who never raised an eyebrow; I watched men grab these same women and drag them into desecrated stores.

My first impulse was to stop and help these innocents, but there were too many for me to make a difference. Too many would-be rapists, too many victims. I was not insensitive to their screams, just helpless. I prayed they would forgive me.

In lieu of that, I prayed I would forgive myself.

It never occurred to me that Gypsy would not be at home. She was always at home. Come hell or high water, she would be in her studio, pouring over an astrological chart, or in her flat, chanting incantations while stroking her purring, black-furred familiar.

When I got to within a block of her apartment, I slowed down and tried to work out an acceptable speech.

"Gypsy, forgive me for I have sinned."

"Gypsy, I'm the biggest asshole God ever created."

"Gypsy, I screwed things up royally."

"Gypsy, take a good crack at me with a cricket racket, then help me stop this terrible mess."

The last contained both revenge and a plea. It was the best I was going to come up with without a serious rewrite.

And I had already edited enough trouble for one lifetime.

Ditching my bike behind some shrubs planted by Lord Marlboro in 1623, I ran the last half block, arriving at the stairs of her flat panting and sweating like a pig. It was the kind of cold perspiration a condemned man feels while waiting for (the former) Governor Bush, of Texas, to pardon him.

Fat chance.

Up the stairs, three at a time, not an easy feat for a man five-foot eightish. Pound on the door, try the knob. Unlocked. Enter, look wildly around. Sniff the air for the lingering scent of incense. Call for the cat.

"Puss, puss, puss."

That cat hated me. I don't know why I bothered. She/he/it knew an infidel when it saw one.

"Gypsy?" And two more times, "Gypsy? Gypsy?" Everything in threes. Then, more tentative, "Gyp? Are you here? It's Kimbo." Then, in a low roar, "Gypsy!"

I went running through the rooms, lingering only briefly at the open bedroom door. Not because I had any particular feelings of arousal at the moment; more from a sake of modesty, though I don't know why. "Modesty" was not a word one cultivates in an orphanage.

"I am here, Andy."

I spun around so fast I almost got friction burn from the air. With a yelp of thankfulness, I spread my arms and ran to her, engulfing her form with the might of a speeding train.

I don't know why I started crying. Maybe it's because I was just glad to find her alive and unhurt. Maybe because I had been afraid the Fates would take her away from me as punishment for my excessive rottenness. Maybe from an overwhelming sense of failure and a deep, abiding desire for forgiveness.

I don't cry easily. I was once pushed out of a boxcar, landing in a tangle of arms and legs. I looked like dog meat and felt as though every nerve in my body had been stripped raw, and never shed a tear. I had been beaten to within an inch of my life by men intent on "saving my soul," and never so much as sniffled. I had been at the top of my profession and plummeted down faster than a 747 carrying exploding oxygen canisters, yet never wept.

So why I bawled like a baby at this point in my life, I'll never know.

Maybe I was making up for lost opportunities. It happens like that sometimes.

"Andy, Andy," Gypsy soothed. "It's all right."

"How can you say that, after what I've done?" And then I remembered: she didn't know what I had done. My tears flowed afresh. "Gypsy, I did it. I gave them the plan to destroy London."

"I know," she softly admitted. I clung to her harder, burying my face under her arm, in case she finished up that line with, "and I'll never forgive you." But she didn't.

Instead, she drew me back, kissed away the tear tracts, then poked the tip of my nose with her finger. I didn't understand the implication of her gesture.

"You're supposed to 'beep' when I do that," she instructed.

"Beep?"

"Yes. Make a beeping noise."

She tried it again.

"Beep?" I said. She smiled approval. "Every time you press my nose, I have to beep?" She nodded. "Does it work in reverse? Do you beep if I press your nose?"

"Try it," she invited. I did. She beeped.

And succeeded in making me smile, despite myself. Sensing I felt better, she grabbed me by the arm. For a moment, I thought I should make another type of noise – a "moo," or a "chug-a-lug" sound, but she had grown serious. I was now ready to listen.

"I do not want you to think about supposed guilt." I started to protest but she stopped me by putting a finger to my lips. I knew what to do with that action. I kissed her. "Neither one of us will think of remorse."

"Neither one of us?" I questioned, but I could see she was in no mood for argument.

"It is now time to undo what we have set in motion."

My shoulders straightened and I cocked my head to better hear her.

"Tell me what to do."

"Write the ending."

"But I already did that," I protested. "Act Four. Fade Out. The End, and all that."

"No," she corrected. "You did not write, 'The End.' I was careful about that."

"All right," I snapped, annoyed at what I perceived to be word games. "But I finished the story."

"You finished Act Four. Now you must write the Tag."

"The Tag?"

"Yes. The short scenario at the end of the play which concludes the work."

"But... how will we implement it? What I created was a blueprint for the Oz Gang. I wrote it, they read it, and then went out an enacted my script. I don't know where they are. And even if I did, I wouldn't be able to make them perform their own destruction."

"You write the ending; what you describe is my part."

I looked down. She was wearing ruby slippers.

"You're the Wicked Witch of the West?" I gasped.

"Something like that," she grinned. I liked the twinkle in her eyes. It spoke of great deviousness.

"OK," I agreed. "I'll write it. But where? On what?"

"I have the answer to that, too." Her smile widened. "You are a reporter, are you not?"

"I am."

"An investigative reporter?"

"I am."

"You have been out in the riots? Witnessed scenes of destruction, first-hand?"

"I have."

"And you planned on writing the story of your life, did you not? Of returning to the CANS Building and writing yourself one hell of a headline?"

I nodded, not bothering to ask why she knew my exact thoughts. You would think I was getting used to having my mind read.

"Yes."

"That is exactly what you shall do."

"Go to the CANS Building and write a story – a tag ending to *Auntie EM?*"

"Now you're cooking with gas!" she articulated in her best Americanese. Which, in all fairness, was better than my best Britishese.

"How do we get there? I only have one bike and besides, CANS is miles – kilometers – away from here."

I didn't even bother to tell her my legs were so sore from peddling, I could barely stand.

She winked at me and twitched her nose in that oh-so familiar Elizabeth Montgomery trademark.

Everything started to go dark. We were FADING OUT....

ACT 15

TAG

FADE IN – EXT. CANS BUILDING - ESTABLISHING SHOT - A NEW DAY

The door is ajar, where looters broke in. Several of the lower windows are
broken. There is an accumulation of trash strewn outside: office equipment, desk
blotters, pencils, pens.

INT. CANS BUILDING - CANS OFFICE - FULL SHOT

Kimbo and Gypsy FADE INTO THE SHOT. In a moment, they are fully materialized.
Kimbo looks around in astonishment.

> KIMBO
> How did we get here?

> GYPSY
> I am the Wicked Witch of the West, remember?
> I have magic powers.

Kimbo REACTS, then shrugs. The time for questioning is over. He looks around.

KIMBO'S POV - THE OFFICE

It has been trashed but not as badly as the lower offices. CAMERA PANS toward
Sweet's office.

CLOSER ANGLE - SWEET'S OFFICE

The door is locked. Everything inside looks untouched.

> KIMBO'S VOICE
> Sweet's office hasn't been broken into.
> (said reverently per
> ever-changing network guidelines)
> Thank God for that! He might forgive
> me for the looting and destruction, but
> never if his keepsakes were trashed.

BACK TO SCENE - FAVORING KIMBO

Kimbo picks his way through the clutter on the floor, goes to his own desk. The
desktop has been messed up but the typewriter is still there. He sits at the desk, inserts a
piece of paper, tries to turn on the power. Nothing happens. He throws up his hands in
frustration.

> KIMBO
> How am I supposed to write when there's
> no juice?

Stepping out from the script pages, I turned to Gypsy, hands on my hips.
"How am I supposed to write when there's no juice?"
"You just said that."

That was in the pink pages I', composing in my head," I complained.

"I suggest you use the typewriter"

"Didn't you just hear me? There's no power. It won't go."

"Have you forgotten about manual typewriters? The staple of the newsroom since shortly after Guttenberg invented the printing press? One of those machines in which you insert a piece of paper and depress keys, which strike a ribbon, leaving an imprint?"

"Where am I going to find one of those?" I demanded. "I know Old Man Poxie is cheap, but we abandoned them *months* ago!"

"Look at your desk."

I looked. There sat my old Royal. It even had my name taped on top. I gasped in hedonistic delight.

"But – it wasn't there a moment ago."

Gypsy impatiently tapped the heels of her red slippers. I scurried over to my desk, sat in my familiar railroad chair – the one with the flat wheels and the squeaks – and shook my shoulders to unknot my muscles. Then, interlacing my fingers, I cracked the joints, reached into the side drawer of my desk, drew out a fresh piece of paper and threaded it through the roller. With a deft unsnap of the lock, I straightened the paper, locked it back into place and began.

TAG, I typed. It read: -A- . I had forgotten to press down hard, and only the "A" came through to the paper.

Being a man of fastidious habits (and also one used to correcting his own typos), I scratched out my mistakes with a pencil eraser miraculously resting in the top drawer, exactly where I always kept one, and began again.

TAG.

I looked for the "Return" key, forgetting this baby wasn't electric. It had been a long times since I hacked away on a manual. (My previous exclamation of *months* being an exaggeration.)

"You might at least have given me an electric typewriter," I complained.

Gypsy gave me one of those "He's really losing it" stares.

"No electricity," she explained.

I had forgotten.

"Right-O."

I banged the Return Bar twice for double-spacing, then started typing. My fingers flew over the keys, sending my emotions back to Yesteryear, and my earliest days as a cub reporter. But, of course here, I was using script format instead of full sentences and paragraphs.

CUT TO:

INT. SCOTLAND YARD - CLOSE ON ROCKET SCIENTIST'S FACE – DAY

He has just read a piece of paper handed him by a subordinate.

                    ROCKET SCIENTIST
          This is it! The information we need.
          Who delivered it?

CAMERA PULLS BACK TO MEDIUM-FULL SHOT, revealing a SUBORDINATE.

The man shakes his head in wonder. He speaks with a SCOTTISH burr.

                    SUBORDINATE
          I don't know, sir. I mean, it didn't make
          any sense.

                    ROCKET SCIENTIST
                    (roaring)
          What do you mean, it didn't make any sense?
          Can't anyone around here speak English? A

man

makes sense; an 'it' doesn't have any to begin
with.

                              SUBORDINATE
                          (defensively)
                    If you had seen them you'd know what I
mean.

                    The message was brought in by some guy
calling

                    himself 'Auntie Em,' and some dame
                    wearing ruby slippers.

                              ROCKET SCIENTIST
                    Jiminy Christmas! A splinter group from
                    the Oz Gang!

    CLOSER ANGLE

    The Chief Inspector re-reads the message. He reacts in a positive
way to what
        he reads.

                          ROCKET   SCIENTIST
(CONT'D)

                    This tells us exactly where the members
                    of the Oz Gang will be. And how to stop
                    them.

                              SUBORDINATE
                          (frightened)
                    How do we know whether or not to
                    believe the message? It may be a trap.

                              ROCKET SCIENTIST

(stiff upper lip)
We have no choice. It's trust this, or
sit back and watch the total destruction
of the planet. We can't survive without
electricity.
(an aside)
Anything is better than giving into their
demands for fiefdoms. You should have heard
what the P.M. said about that.

SUBORDINATE
I don't know why he was so upset, sir.
Only last season, the Queen's List had a
dog catcher and a hairdresser on it.

Rocket Scientist makes a LOW, DISPARAGING NOISE under his breath.

ROCKET SCIENTIST
Politics   are   not   our   business,   Harris-
Dumphree!

Call in the boys. Cancel everyone's leave. I
want all of our officers in on this.

SUBORDINATE
But you know what the P.M. said about
overtime....

ROCKET SCIENTIST
(profound)
The Fate of the World is at stake.
We can't worry about pounds and shillings
at a time like this!

FAVORING SUBORDINATE

Glad, for once, he's not the Chief Inspector.

HARD   CUT
TO:

Gypsy and I were there at the denouement. It was my duty, after all, being an investigative reporter. The Fate of the World hung in the balance. How could I explain to Sweet I wrote the concluding scenes, but didn't cover them?

I set it where it began – at the mansion and erstwhile headquarters of Auntie EM. The entire gang was all there, sans the Scarecrow: Dorothy, the Wizard, Tin Man, Cowardly Lion and Toto. They were gathered in the den, just cracking the cork on a bottle of aged Perrier. Wizard held up his Star of Edinburgh champagne glass.

"I believe a toast is in order," he declared, his eyes as bubbly as the naturally carbonated spring water. "To Auntie EM – long may she reign."

"To Dorothy, long may she reign," Dorothy corrected.

Tin Man did the honors of pouring the bubbly. He did not give himself any. It was bad for his constitution; rusted his insides something fierce.

"It has all come to pass," Lion continued, sipping his "brew." "Exactly as we envisioned it. Mass destruction, without bombs. Without land mines. Princess Di would be proud. No bloodshed."

That was my cue. I stepped out from behind the curtains draped by the floor-to-ceiling windows.

"Without bloodshed?" I demanded. They turned to me, startled.

"Where'd you come from?" Toto demanded. My entrance was a serious breach of etiquette. I had not even been announced.

"I'm Auntie Em, remember? The 'mother' to you all. And Mother is not pleased."

They appeared disconcerted. It was bred deep into the fibre of all blue-bloods to respect their mother.

"You're not our mother – you're only an aunt," Dorothy protested. But I could see she was wavering.

"I'm your adopted mother. With all the legal rights and obligations of a birth parent."

I was on safe ground here. I had researched it once, when I thought I might be adopted. I continued before I was forced to explain.

"You took over London, but it was hardly without bloodshed. Or death. Remember your late, unlamented co-conspirator? The Scarecrow? He, with the pacemaker? You killed him by shutting off the battery which ran his heart.

"And what about the mass hysteria created by your little parlor trick? You turned a civilization crazy. Looting, rape, fist-fights. The weak, the young and the old and the defenseless were all trampled or beaten to death. Without power, patients in hospitals died. Without electricity to regulate the highways and byways, motor vehicles ran into one another at high speeds, killing the drivers and passengers. Without Law and Order, citizens ran amok."

The Cowardly Lion took exception to my graphic details.

"But we're going to step in and re-regulate all that. Once we unite our kingdoms we'll take over Great Britain. Leaving out Northern Ireland, of course. Two queens and three kings."

Dorothy cut him off.

"One queen and four palatines," she amended.

This time, the Lion was not to be put off.

"About that," he said, turning to their leader. "I say we're all in on this equally. Slavery was abolished in the 1800s. "There are four of us, and we should all be kings and queens."

"There are *five* of us," Toto growled. "Don't leave me out."

The Cowardly Lion was ready for her.

"You're only a dog," he informed the irate actress.

"Who you calling a dog, you dammed lion! You're not so handsome, yourself," she snarled.

"Please! Let us have decorum!" interrupted the Tin Man. Both turned on him.

"You don't have a heart, so stay out of it!" they demanded in perfect unison.

"Lady and gentleman," Wizard offered, trying to live up to his second billing. Unfortunately, those under the title held little sway and he had little success quelling the argument. Dorothy finished him off with an ingénue's flair for the dramatic.

"Never mind about you," Dorothy snapped. "You're a phony, remember? The man with all the flashing lights and colored smoke, but no substance? You're the one who flew away in your hot air balloon and left me behind! I only included *you* in this group because you said you were a writer. But you couldn't even spell! That's why we had to bring *him* in," she said, pointing an accusing finger at me.

All eyes turned in my direction. I bashfully smiled.

"That's my middle name: Andy Good-Speller Kimbo. Say," I realized, noting the significance of my new name. "I'm a hyphenate, too!"

They were not impressed. So much for blue blood.

Wizard pushed Dorothy back. Infuriated, she balled her fist and took a swing at him. He sidestepped her punch and it landed on the Tin Man. I swear I heard a resounding PING.

"You can't hurt me," he jeered.

She threw her imported water into his chest and he immediately rusted in place.

Sensing her big scene, Toto bared her teeth and charged the Lion. Being the coward that he was, he tucked tail between legs and fled the room, there to be grabbed by the unseen, waiting men from Scotland Yard which I had so carefully scripted into place.

That left Dorothy, Wizard and Toto as the heirs-apparent to the throne and all the riches promised by Auntie EM. You've heard of the expression, "an heir and a spare"? Apparently the two "humans" were familiar with it, as well, for they turned in unison on the "dog." Sensing her imminent danger, Toto shook her head while riffling her ruff.

"Stay away from me," she warned, to no good effect. Give her credit: she sized up the situation and tried for a "man's best friend" approach. Although, in this case, it was a "woman's best friend."

"Dorothy, I'm your companion; your pet. I came all the way from Kansas with you. *I'll* never steal power from you. Not like that conniving trickster."

All eyes turned to Wizard. He shook his head while putting distance between himself and the wannabe's from RADA. When he spoke, it was in a deep, rumbly voice, augmented, somehow, to imitate the Know-It-All from the movie.

"I am the Wizard of Oz." And then, almost sarcastically, "In the land of Oz, the Wizard is king."

So saying, he tossed a pellet onto the floor. It broke upon impact, enveloping the three characters in a cloud of swirling red smoke.

There were sounds of grunts, groans, snarls, unintelligible curses (it was supposed to be a family flick, after all. Blood and guts OK, swearing *verboten*), and sundry thuds. The smoke was too thick for me to see or to have a clue who might turn out the winner. My instinct was on Dorothy, but I was betting on the Wizard, with Toto coming in with the long odds.

I had failed to count on the dark horse. When all was said and done and the red smoke cleared, it was the Wicked Witch who stood triumphant over all.

"Gypsy!" I cried in joy.

She smiled and took a bow.

"Never underestimate the power of the West," she drawled in Cowboyese. "Right, Pardner?"

"Right!" I happily agreed, silently promising the gods of the Grade B Western never to turn off another Gene Autry oater.

"Time to ride off into the sunset, before the boys with the 'S.Y.' branding irons come to gather up what's left of their yearling cattle," she concluded.

"Hi, YO," I agreed, holding out my hand. She accepted it and we rode off into the sunset, which, in this play, happened to be through the window.

No sooner had my feet touched the outside soil, when everything

FADED TO BLACK.

When my head cleared, the lights had come up. Literally.

I was back in the study, seated behind the desk, my FINGERs poised over the keys of the typewriter. The electric machine emitted a low hum of power. The Oz Gang – all six of them – were standing in exactly the same places they had been, before we set out on our Great unWar to End All Wars.

"What the hell?" the reincarnated Paul Wiedenmyer exclaimed, raising a trembling hand to his sweaty forehead.

"What have you done?" Eleanor Andress asked me, her voice a whisper of what it had been.

"No more and no less than what you asked of him," a familiar voice exclaimed. We all turned toward the curtained windows, as Gypsy, still wearing the red ruby slippers, emerged from her hiding place.

"You!" Timothy Button-Rhoades cried.

"I – we – know you from someplace," the former Scarecrow exclaimed.

"You were in the – dream," Noel Delaney clarified.

"The Wicked Witch of the West," Mary Keswick concluded. "In Act Two of *Auntie EM*, it was Glinda, the Wonderful Witch of the East, who had the house fall on her."

"I am the Gypsy," Gypsy corrected. "I – and Mister Kimbo – have given you Act Four and the concluding tag sequence of your play.

With a little help from Auntie EM." They stared at her in dumbfounded wonder. "There is a scientific theory that a very powerful magnetic field can alter time; making ripples through which one may pass. You unwittingly supplied me with the wherewithal to prove that theory. By activating your 'Auntie EM' device to full power – which you had never done before – it opened up passages into another dimension. Following the script Mr. Kimbo wrote, you lived the consequences of a world being destroyed. It was not a 'dream,' Mr. Cowardly Lion, it was a… dress rehearsal."

She paused to stare at the wide-eyed, open-mouthed faces trying to absorb what she was saying.

"A real one, I grant you, complete with 'audience' participation. So, you have all had a glimpse of what your bloodless war would look like. Was it what you expected?"

The wannabe thespians exchanged glances.

"Not for me," Pail Wiedenmyer stated with reverence. "I ended up dying before I got to enjoy it."

"Did the rest of you enjoy it?" Gypsy asked, using his ill-chosen expression. "You read the script. You knew what was going to happen. Although," she confessed, pointing at the Scarecrow, "bits of it were extemporized."

None of them dared offer an affirmation, having found reality somewhat different than playacting.

"By turning off Auntie EM," Gypsy continued, "time reasserted itself and the alternate dimension closed, reverting everything back to the moment before the window opened. Thus, you find yourselves here with the opportunity to… abandon your acting careers."

"You – tricked us," Eleanor began, but Gypsy cut her off.

"Not a trick. You saw one version of the future. You have been granted the gift of insight."

"We can abandon Auntie EM and go back to living out real lives?" the Wizard choked.

"That is up to you," Gypsy evenly replied.

"But," Dorothy tried, furiously debating her options, "I might have been queen."

"That would be the sequel," Gypsy reminded her. "Which has yet to be written. Give Mr. Kimbo another day or two and see what he devises for your fate."

"I'll write it, myself."

Gypsy clucked her tongue. A gesture undoubtedly picked up from watching too much late night television.

"You and Mr. Polle have been replaced as the head writers. By anointing him to create the ending, the characters now belong to him and he has the first right of refusal on the sequel."

"Refuse," she demanded, glowering at me. "Or, write as I dictate."

"Sorry, Ms. Andress, but I don't need a collaborator and I won't be your ghost writer. I see it all, clearly." I spread my arms wide, envisioning the scene. "London is nearly destroyed by the looting and the panic. But, Her Majesty, the Queen, holds steadfast. Just as her father did during World War II. She calls for tranquility; sets the example by going out in the street and directing the ambulance corps. Charles redesigns the new architecture which will replace those buildings destroyed and torn down. Prince Philip will walk the corgis, reminding everyone to pick up the poo left by their own pets. The term 'doggie bag' will take on an entirely new meaning."

My mind's eye sketched it for me as though I were really creating a new world.

"London will recover, beginning a new Age of prosperity for the British Isles. M16 will track down those who called themselves Auntie EM. You will all be arrested and tried for high crimes and misdemeanors. Barristers wearing wigs and black robes, harkening back to the days when Charles Laughton set the standard in *Witness for the Prosecution,* will try and convict you. You'll all be sent to the Tower where you can look out on the spikes where so many traitors once hung. You, Dorothy," I charged, warming to the subject, "will request an axe man from France. Unfortunately for you, the precedent set by Henry VIII will be ignored and your plea will be denied. On appeal, it will be decided the best way to execute you six will be by turning Auntie EM to a limited-area frequency that will... blow your minds. You'll get off easy," I parenthetically noted for the Scarecrow, "as your pacemaker will fail before you ever make it to the ultimate trip."

I intended to scare them and I succeeded. I saw an Antoinette Perry award in my future.

Timothy Button-Rhoades held up his hands in surrender.

"All right. You win. How do we get out of this?"

"Go. Leave this house and never come back. Depart as six grammar school thespians who once wrote, but failed to perform, a graduation play called *Auntie Em.* That will be the end of it."

"And if we don't?"

That, from Dorothy.

"I told you what I'm going to write. Settle for the bad review of what might have happened and find some other way to amuse yourselves. Try getting a job. You'll be amazed how much of your time it takes up. You won't have a free moment to rue your failed plot to assume control over the world. And, at least, you'll be alive."

As they say in the theatre, the actors took their curtain calls and gracefully bowed out.

"You mean, I didn't really let my ego get the better of me?" I asked, swinging my leg over the arm of Gypsy's rocking chair and settling in with the strong cup of coffee she had just handed me. I was feeling pretty good about myself and how Gypsy and I had Saved the World.

"You lived through what happened," she evasively replied.

"Then I *did* write it," I pouted.

"You also wrote the death and destruction which followed," she reminded me. I was hardly appeased.

"Humbling," I admitted.

"Absolute power corrupts absolutely," she reminded me.

"A truism I was never particularly fond of," I admitted. "But will take stock of in future."

"And stick to reporting," she agreed.

"Holy Cow!" I exclaimed, slapping my hand on my knee and incidentally spilling coffee over my pants. "I promised Sweet a story. What am I going to write?"

"Exactly what happened."

"What happened? But – it didn't happen. I mean –"

"You investigated a series of seemingly related instances concerning loss of electrical power, concluding –"

"It's the Curse of Civilization," I finished with a sigh. She smiled contentedly. "Not exactly the Pulitzer Prize winning byline I envisioned."

"But it will make Mr. McGraw very happy."

"That is not my goal in life."

"What is?" she asked less innocently than it sounded.

I rested my head back against the back of the chair and closed my eyes. It was all as clear as if I were peering through another dimension.

INT. GYPSY'S FLAT - MEDIUM SHOT - KIMBO AND GYPSY – NIGHT

Soft, romantic MUSIC plays in the b.g. A black cat PURRS contentedly.

CLOSER ANGLE - FAVORING KIMBO

He makes eye contact with Gypsy. She smiles at his unspoken invitation.

CAMERA pulls back and PANS them as they grasp hands. Electricity CRACKLES
   in the air.

(FIRST REVISION) Emotion SPARKLES in the air.

FULL SHOT

Kimbo and Gypsy move toward the bedroom, pause at the door and kiss. It is
a long, stimulating kiss. HOLD, then they slip through the doorway into the
BLACK interior.

INTERIOR BEDROOM - ANGLE ON FLOOR

Clothes shed in haste.

CLOSE SHOT – BED

Kimbo and Gypsy making mad, wild love. They will remain in this furious
embrace for hours, days, months. They are the champions, the King and Queen
of Passion. (As opposed to the queen and king of Oz.)

Well, I'm writing this, aren't I? Who says I don't have a vivid imagination?

Gypsy takes Kimbo's hand and as the MUSIC RISES to a crescendo the SCENE BLURS.

FADE OUT.

TAG

FADE IN:

INT. GYPSY'S FLAT - ANGLE ON BED - KIMBO AND
GYPSY – NIGHT

Sometime later. Both are sweaty, glowing from their recently-concluded
lovemaking. There is more to come.

> GYPSY
> The most wonderful thing happened
> to me.

> KIMBO
> (dreamily)
> To me, too, lover.

> GYPSY
> I shall frame it.

Kimbo sits up in bed, rubs his eyes. Looks down at his partially covered
anatomy.

> KIMBO
> Don't you think you better leave it
> where it is?

> GYPSY
> My letter.

> KIMBO
> They give letters for varsity love making?

> GYPSY

From the reporter at the <u>Post Dispatch;</u>
the newspaper in St. Louis.

                    KIMBO
                (somewhat shocked)
        They covered our bedroom activities?
        Who let them in? Are there photographs?

                    GYPSY
        Thanking me for my generous
        donation to the "Light the Arch
        Campaign."

CLOSE – KIMBO

Reacting - hard (figuratively speaking). He considers, then pulls
the bedclothes nearer his chin.

                    GYPSY
        My letter says that the response has been
        so enthusiastic, the Arch will be lit
        by Christmas.

                    KIMBO
                    (dryly)
        I'd like to be 'lit' at Christmas, too.

                    GYPSY
        Think of all the new photographs for
        the Missouri calendars: The Arch lit for the
holidays.

        The Arch lit from the St. Louis side. The
        Arch lit from the Illinois side. The lighted
        Arch as seen from an airplane. The

lighted Arch as seen from a photographer lying on the ground. The lighted Arch viewed from Highway 40 while stuck in morning rush hour!

Who was it who said writers have it all their own way?

FADE OUT (AGAIN).

THE END

AUTHOR'S NOTE

Dear faithful readers and especially those who love a puzzle. Not a "Who Done It," but rather those with an eye toward what we, in the Business, call "continuity mistakes." You know what I mean. Like when you're watching the super spy choose which agents to include in his present caper but something catches your eye and you're not sure what's wrong. You can't solve the mystery until you buy the DVD and rewind the scene several times before finally catching on. The fish in the aquarium behind the lead actor are *swimming backwards*. Is this a subliminal code that will have great significance in Act Four? Probably not.

Or, the ever popular cigar which starts as a five-inch Stogie in one scene, has been reduced to a stub a moment later and by the third shot, it's some size midway between the two. The same goes for ashes. Has the character lit, relit, stubbed out and changed brands while investigating the crime? None of the above.

The first instance was actually a *purposeful mistake* because the editor is using footage from a previous episode to save time and money. Unfortunately, in the original, correct version, the actor is selecting the photograph from the lead guest star, but in the second, a photograph of a different star has to be substituted. To get the angles correct, the super spy has to face the proper direction, even if that means flipping, or *reversing* the film. Sharp-eyed buffs will also catch this trick being performed when, in close-up, an actor is staring to his right watching the outlaws ride away, when in the Master, or Full Shot, he's looking to his left. Since it would be too expensive to bring the actor back to re-shoot the scene, the matching mistake is fixed by reversing the film, thus changing the direction he's looking from east to west. You can confirm your suspicion by checking which side his hair (real or toupee) is parted on. Or, if he's wearing a cowboy hat and you can't tell, look at which side his shirt is buttoned on.

And you always wondered why men's and women's shirts buttoned on different sides. Forget the sword scabbard theory. It's actually a joke created by ancient wizards or mischievous elves to muddle the concept of movie magic. Or, to paraphrase the *character* of Ed Wood, it destroys the suspension of disbelief.

In any case, matching mistakes are *never* blamed on the director. They're attributed to the (almost universally) uncredited, and always underpaid and overworked "script girl," whose job it is to catch matching mistakes (including dialogue fluffs), chart all the scenes shot per day, make certain everything is ready for the next day's shoot, type everything up my morning, *and* carry aspirin in her pocket for those who show up with hangovers.

I know, Count Dracula. I know too much to live. And now, you do, too.

As noted in my previous two tomes, which you've all read, thank you very much, I mentioned my journalistic adventures (High Dramas with overtones of Humor), are set in or around 1984, but due to circumstances beyond my control, some references to events happening in the future invariably slipped in. That's because, as you already know, translating my work notes into readable text was done at a later date. Rather than remove them (a prodigious amount of research and re-writing would have to be done, resulting in the proverbial "pink pages"), I decided to present them as a challenge to you, my beloved readers.

You know the cartoon that runs in the newspapers where the artist creates two panels, the second one slightly altered from the first, and you have to find all the differences? That's the way I want you to look at this. Go through the text and see if you can find all the – not "errors," exactly – but purposeful transgressions. (HINT: more than a few have to do with America's Pastime.) Then, drop me a line and we can compare lists.

After all, reading is supposed to make you think, as well as entertain, right?

A Kimbo

P.S. In the above typed signature, kindly forgive the double space between "A" and Kimbo. On these modern day computers, the designers of word processing software invariably think the users are idiots (doofuses, jerks, uneducated fools), and they incorporate *inviolate* Rules, one of them being that if you start a sentence with a Capital A followed by a period, you're making a list rather than typing a name, and thus the double space. Just try to take that extra space away, I dare you. What happens is that you get A.Kimbo (no space) or it removes the "A" altogether, leaving Kimbo.

Being none of the above (including idiot, doofus, jerk or an uneducated fool), I resent this.

Also, I can't repair it.

P.P.S. I add this last so you won't count the double space as a mistake or a typo on the list you're going to send me.

P.P.P.S.

Again, I was forced to make a choice with my initials. This time I opted for no spaces.

P.P.P.P.S.

This manuscript ends with the inevitable "GSFE," inserted by my ghostwriters. You can write me about that, too, and I'll tell you the secret.

Maybe.

K.

GSFE

ALSO BY: S.L.KOTAR AND J.E.GESSLER

"The Hugh Kerr Mystery Series"..

The Conundrum of
- I   **The Decapitated Detective**
- II   **The Absconded Attorney**
- III   **The Sins of the Fathers**
- IV   **The Two-Sided Lawyer**
- V   **The Clueless Counselor**
- VI   **The Loveless Marriage**
- VII   **The Executed Defendant**
- VIII   **The Jettisoned Jury**
- IX   **The Perjured Pigeon**
- X   **The Haunting Halloween Party**
- XI   **The Tuneless Tunesmith**
- XII   **The Meddling Motorcar**
- XIII   **The Blundering Bear**
- XIV   **The Shooting Fish in a Barrel**
- XV   **The Girl with the Emerald Eyes**
- XVI   **The Vanishing Cream**
- XVII   **The Convoluted Confession**
- XVIII   **The Skeleton in the Closet**

"New Beginnings Series"

- I   **The Believer**
- II   **The Heretic**
- III   **Arrow Song**
- IV   **Peas In A Pod**
- V   **The Agnostics**

" The Kimbo – Stop the Presses! – Series

- One   **Mystic Seer**
- Two   **I am the News**
- Three   **Antie EM**

- Four   **Ashes to Ashes and all that Jazz**

"the ReproBate saga"

- I   **Beneath the Rose**
- II   **skull and cRossBones**
- III   **Redefining Bastions**
- IV   **thicker than Blood**
- V   **prioR Battles**
- VI   **Requited Blasphemy**
- VII   **The waR Between**
- VIII   **To Richmond or Bust**
- IX   **carrying Battlescars**
- X   **RamBlings**
- XI   **Retrieving Ballast**
- XII   **captain's RB**
- XIII   **wondeRous Backdrops**
- XIV   **ReproBate**
- XV   **time and tRouBle**
- XVI   **the Road Back**
- XVII   **oveR the Brink**

"the Hellhole saga"

- I   **First Draw**
- II   **Audition for a Legend**
- III   **Strange Bedfellows**
-

"The Kansas Pirate Series"

- I   **Pirate Treasure**
- II   **Strawberry Fields**
- III   **The Drinking Gourd**

- **Catman**

- **ONE**

- **Shepherd of the Kingdom**

- **Wolf Eyes**

- **I Am the Ship**

- **Blue Moon**

- **Target'd**

- **Star Bright**

Non-Fiction
"**The Kepi Magazine,**" :
- **Volume I and II**
- **Volumes III and IV**

www.ingramcontent.com/pod-product-compliance
Lightning Source LLC
Chambersburg PA
CBHW060150130626
46556CB00006B/2578